THE MAKER'S QUEST

(A CYRUS ROVER ADVENTURE)

A story about stories.

**Walk through the door and join Cyrus on
this life-changing adventure.**

RUSS MATTHEWS

*I think it's what art should do: make you feel less alone - either in the quest for truth
or in dealing with any pain you have. — Brendan Gleeson*

This publication is designed to provide accurate and authoritative information regarding the subject matter covered. It is sold with the understanding that the author or publisher is not engaged in rendering legal, accounting, or other professional services. If legal advice or other expert assistance is required, the services of a competent professional person should be sought.

ISBN: 978-0-6468942-1-8

Printed in Australia and the United States of America

To Delores and Ron Matthews, mentoring always came naturally for you.

CONTENTS

YOUR FREE GIFT

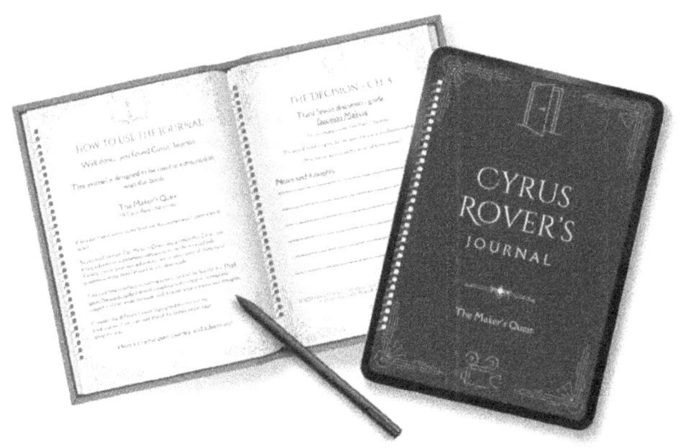

As a thank you for purchasing this book, we'd love to gift you a copy of Cyrus' Journal. Inside you'll find space to record your thoughts and a-ha's as you read through the book.

Get your copy here: https://thirdspace.org.au/cyrus or scan the QR code.

PRAISE FOR THE MAKER'S QUEST

"This book offers a unique take on a familiar motif. With traces of A Christmas Carol, glimpses of The Matrix and even a foray into Narnia, Russ Matthews reveals his heart for cinema and his heart for those seeking truth. Through this story, he reminds us that our quest for achievement should be eclipsed by something greater - sacrifice."

~ Max Jeganathan - Senior Research Fellow, Centre for Public Christianity (CPX)

"People have been attempting to share about who God is and how He desires to interact with us from the poetry of Job to the parables of Jesus. Russ has an incredible knack of creating a Third Space to capture the stories people long to tell and connect them to the One who started the Story from the beginning."

~ Tim Weihrauch - Metro Community Church - Vadalia Campus Pastor & So You Want To Be in Ministry podcast

"I loved it! Russ brings out the beauty of the journey of faith through Cyrus Rover's action packed and romantic journey of faith. I felt I was in the hospital room with him."

~ Ashley Wilson - Power to Change

"The Maker's Quest takes you on a unique journey with Cyrus Rover, while engaging with important topics like relationships, decisions, self sacrifice and more, all while keeping The Maker at center stage. I look forward to seeing how God will use this book to help the readers ask the tough questions of life."

~ Pastor Matt Reno - Nevada Baptist Church

FOREWORD

"*Stories kind of sneak up on us*". Like music and songs, stories get past our guard. They get under our skin, because they tap into our imagination, our emotions, our longings, our fears and our dreams. Throughout history, every tribe and culture have had stories at the heart of their communal life. Stories create culture, and community, they hold us together, whether they are told around a cooking fire, written on parchment or shown on the big screen.

Stories are a way of making us think, of teaching us wisdom in a way that straight statements or propositions can't do. They invite us into the lives of other people, real or in vivid imagination. In fact, when the greatest of all teachers wanted to teach truths that would cross cultures and cross centuries, he told us stories; stories that still impact our culture, like 'the prodigal son', or 'the good Samaritan'. These stories have shaped the lives of millions.

In almost all traditional cultures, stories were used to teach wisdom to young people; understanding is necessary for them to live productive lives that will bless others. We might call this process of being taught - *initiation*.

Richard Rohr, in his book, 'Adam's Return', speaks of the patterns of initiation in ancient cultures, to bring into adulthood (in his book particularly into young manhood). Richard tells of the five hard truths that the young need to learn, namely; life is hard; you are not that important; your life is not about you; you're not in control; and you're going to die. It's these hard truths that need to be personally, deeply understood, give real wisdom for life, for both men and women. In fact it's an irony that in learning that "life is really not all about you", that we can be set free from the prison that is "selfishness".

In 'The Maker's Quest' Russ Matthews has combined these two threads. The quest is a story of initiation, a kind of spiritual initiation where a young man learns some difficult but essential truths. It's about the learning of wisdom, the understanding of self, and the purpose of life, told in a story about stories. The quest is a journey through stories told in films, that so many of us have loved, as we've walked with characters who have been a part of our lives and imaginations.

Cyrus Rover travels and learns from these characters who brought joy to the lives of so many people, young and old, as he learns the meaning and purpose of life. He comes to understand the beautiful mystery at the centre of life, and the way to find that life, by knowing the one who is the author of life itself.

This is a story you can enjoy because at one level it's a fantasy, and it's a journey through characters that are old friends, and yet it's also a parable of the spiritual journey we are all on in life. At the end this quest will make us think about where we are in our spiritual journey, and do we know the one who gives us life itself.

~ Al Stewart, author of *The Manual: Getting Masculinity Right*

GET THE DISCUSSION GUIDES

To make the most out of this book, we've created a number of 'discussion guides' that will help you with certain concepts inside the book. To access those, simply scan the QR code below (or visit this link here https://thirdspace.org.au/collection/9391).

1

THE LIFE OF CYRUS ROVER

My bike chain fell off again today.

Ugh, I do my best to make it to work on time, but every day seems to be a struggle. All I want to do is try to get ahead of my life, but it always feels like something is working against me.

It only takes a minute to get the chain back on the drive-wheel, and I'm able to get off to work. The whole thing puts me in a foul mood, though. I charge through the city streets without much regard for pedestrians or cars, which gets me some nasty looks and creative verbal responses to my riding. Wow, I didn't know you could use those words as nouns, verbs, *and* adjectives.

All I can do is think of how Phil will roll his eyes as I get into the cafe late - again. Yesterday he lectured me on the value of promptness and how there were others who wanted my job. Mentally, I shook my head because I knew that no one else wanted to work at this place. The café was tucked back behind alleyways that used to be cool a decade earlier, but now looked pretty tired. It was a miracle anyone found it. Still, I needed the job and didn't have the time to look for something better right now.

As I pedal through the footpaths and side streets, the whole world seems angry with me and I'm riding like the world is my greatest enemy. I guess we deserve one another. A taxi driver gives me the finger, a businessman yells at me as I accidentally splash him, and even a homeless guy gets into the action and throws a rock at me as I rush down the street. Looking back at this guy with only one shoe on, matted dreadlocks, and a plaid blanket covering his shoulders, I neglected to see the delivery truck backing out of a side street that ran alongside an apartment complex on Jefferson Street.

I slammed into the side of Carletti's fruit truck. There was the crumpling of my bike tire and a flash of red paint on the side panel. Then my head crashed into the company logo, and that is the last thing I remember.

I wake up in a school that could be set in the 1950s. That is when I notice I'm sitting at a desk wearing a school uniform that has a patch on the jacket. I look around at the students sitting in the classroom. Most are wearing the same jackets, while others' jackets are on their desk chairs. Each student has a starched white shirt, a tie, and everyone looks bored.

Suddenly, I realize that there is a teacher at the front of the classroom who looks like someone from the 50s or 60s. It might have been because I had just watched The Dead Poet's Society, but he looked different enough. He could have been any of the teachers from a film based in that era. He is leafing through a book as one of the other students reads the introduction to a chapter on poetry. Interestingly, the same textbook is open on my desk. As I check out what everyone else was doing in the room, I listen to the dialogue between the instructor and his students. Then I come to my wits and know where I am sitting.

What was going on? I remember hitting the side of the delivery truck, and now I'm on the set of something that was similar to the classic film my friends and I had been watching last night.

***

Doctor's notes

Cyrus Rover, 18-year-old male. Bicycle accident. Facial lacerations. A few of his fingers are broken and a broken right arm. He arrived unconscious and unresponsive. All of his other vitals are normal. Yet, no response to stimuli, and breathing is erratic. He has some eye movement, but otherwise, he seems to have slipped into a coma-like state.

"Should he remain in the ICU for now?" Sylvia Bloodworth asked. She was a 3rd-year intern and had seen this sort of thing before, but she needed to confirm things with the hospital's head of medicine.

Doctor J. Rashid was on call that evening. He looked intense, with a hint of concern in his voice.

"Spinal injuries?"

Sylvia shook her head.

"No. Miraculously. But no response to any stimuli."

The seasoned physician looked down on the young man in the bed. He could see that he was fit, but it looked like he hadn't slept much lately and, like many students, was slightly malnourished. Even if his face was a bit of a mess right now. Cyrus was not a name you heard too often. The biker reminded him of someone.

"Let's keep him in the ICU for observation for the next 24 hours, then let's see if he responds soon. Surprising that he would remain unresponsive. Keep an eye on him and update me if there are any changes. Make sure to get a CAT scan done. Any relatives for Mr. Rover?"

"We're still looking into his records. Nothing yet," Sylvia replied. "He seems to be from out of state. I'll keep you updated, Doctor."

The intern knew the routine, but still felt for this young man. The details in his bag showed that he was a film student at City University. Cyrus had a laptop, phone and a notebook with the University's logo on it. He even had a couple of DVDs.

Who still watches DVDs? the young doctor wondered.

She had tried to find some details about his family, but nothing yet.

The team of doctors moved on to the next patient.

***

This all had to be a dream, but it seemed so real. The smell of the school, the uniform and the classroom made it all feel like it was happening in real time.

"Mr Rover. I have a question for you."

The distinguished man was looking straight at me over the top of his glasses. His tweed suit with patches on the elbows conveyed that he was an academic, but his eyes gave off a larrikin spirit hidden underneath the stodgy exterior.

His question made me sit up straight in my desk chair.

"Yes, um... sir. I'm sorry, could you repeat the question?"

The teacher looked confused.

"I'm sorry. I told the class at the beginning of the term. 'Sir' isn't necessary. You can call me Mr. Elijah. Not sure where the 'sir' aspect is coming from, Mr Rover. My question is how does poetry reflect life?"

Suddenly, I felt like things took an odd turn. Was this a dream, was it real or was I merely in the story? I must have looked confused.

Mr. Elijah had a small grin on his face.

"Mr Rover. Focus on what I'm asking you. I need you to answer this question. How do poetry and art reflect your life?"

The rest of the class was looking at me now, and the teacher had stood up with this second request for an answer. At this point, I knew I needed to respond.

Poetry, art, my life? What's going on?

2

CYRUS ROVER'S BACKSTORY

Up until my bike crashed into that truck, my life was pretty unremarkable. I grew up in a middle-class family. Living on the city's outskirts was the most exciting portion of my life. If there was anything that differentiated me from my friends in high school, it was that I was raised by my grandparents, Les and Katy Fremont. They were good, church-going people from a different era. My mother had passed away when I was young. Grandma had done all she could to care for me over the years. My dad hadn't really been part of my life. The only thing I inherited from him was my last name, Rover. Yeah, I did get crap about the name, but since I was constantly on the move as a child, it kinda fitted.

Most of my friends called me Cy, but my grandmother called me Cyrus. She was great, and so was my grandfather, even though he was a man of few words. Les worked with his hands, and he had raised three daughters. He wasn't as keen to invest in my life when I came along. I don't know if it was grief or tiredness from hard work. Still, he loved me and made sure I had everything I needed.

On the other end of the spectrum was my Grandma Katy, who wanted to be involved in everything. If I was doing something, she would support me, whether I wanted her there or not. Despite feeling a bit smothered at times, I knew my grandmother was there for me whenever I needed her. Amazing woman, she acted like she was 20 years younger than she actually was. She sacrificed her 'retirement' season of life for me. She wasn't heavy-handed in anything, but there was one thing Gram Kat required while living with her. I had to go to church on Sunday.

As a child raised by grandparents, church was a constant through the good times and the bad times. We went through a few pastors, some good, some, well, okay. The standout was Pastor Hudson, who invested in the church, loved the people and even liked the unruly kid in the back pews. Nothing creepy. He just watched out for me and made sure I learned the Bible and got some extra attention from an older man since my dad wasn't on the scene.

If I excelled in anything in high school, besides girls and bicycles, it was filming things. Grandpa Les had an old video camera he let me have as a child. From that day, things were never the same.

I filmed everything. That old camera was attached to me and managed to fit in my backpack for years. Of course, I started upgrading as I got older. If people asked what I wanted for a gift, it was always film equipment. Not clothes, not sports equipment. Naw, filming equipment was my go-to.

Even though they didn't understand, my grandparents did enjoy watching my bizarre creations. They laughed, cried, and sometimes corrected me when I filmed something they thought was inappropriate. Girls seemed a regular subject, but I did venture out and film other things. The church even benefited from my skills, I became their audio/visual guy for years. It was one thing that Pastor Hudson always appreciated about me. It also meant he could ask me about life and my spiritual walk. I may not have shown it outwardly, but he was pretty cool, for a pastor.

There was another thing that my grandparents loved about this side of my life: movies. We watched so many movies. At the theater, at home. We watched a movie most nights after the nightly news. Old, new, foreign, arthouse – it didn't matter. We would watch 'em all. It really brought us together. We would talk about them for hours afterward, and it was one of the rare moments when I would get words out of Grandpa Les.

So, it was no surprise that I enrolled at film school in the city, and my grandparents visited every once in a while, even though it was across the state line. City University was one of the best in the country and life in the big city was different from home. It was an intense program and my schedule was all over the place since our projects involved events at all times of the day.

Honestly, I loved the bizarre nature of my world, even though it didn't leave much time for a social life. Especially once I started factoring in my days at the café, my existence amounted to work and film school. I loved it, except for my cash-strapped lifestyle. I lived the role of a starving artist but it made me hungry for my craft.

Don't get me wrong, I still enjoyed flirting with any young woman who entered my orbit. Come on, I'm a red-blooded male who looks at the world through a camera lens. As my youth pastor said once during one of those awkward sex and the Bible talks, one of God's greatest creations was women. It proved that God was an artist with a wonderful eye for beauty. And He had certainly gifted men with eyes to see them. Our hands needed to have permission before touching, though. I did *hear* the message of the talk, but I didn't always follow the rules. But there wasn't much time or money to spend on dates. So, I did all I could to find myself in situations where I could meet young women at university and work. It was always fun to flirt.

At work, I had a friend named Mika. We enjoyed talking during the slow hours. She was a student at the University too and was focusing on the sound engineering side of things. Her background was Japanese, but she had grown up in the city. Her parents had migrated from Japan when she was a baby. So, she connected with her heritage but didn't live like she was from there. Even though she did have an affinity for Japanese cinema and Studio Ghibli animation. We loved talking about film productions and our dreams. She was gorgeous, except we were both time-poor and financially strapped. So, we just enjoyed a friendship even though there seemed to be chemistry between us.

On day I hit the truck, I was thinking of a project I was doing on a retrospective of Peter Weir films. The Australian director was a favorite of my professor. I had watched Dead Poets Society with Mika and a couple of other friends. We had stayed up late talking about the project and how sad it was to lose Robin Williams.

As everyone was leaving my place, Mika gave me a peck on the cheek. Honestly, I wanted to grab her right there and give her a more dedicated kiss. But, with everyone around, it wasn't appropriate. It did get me thinking about her all night, though. That is probably why I forgot to set my alarm.

***

I sat there in the classroom trying to register what was happening around me. The teacher asking about art? All I could think was that Mika would love this, whatever this is.

I was rudely jolted out of my thoughts when I heard the teacher's voice again.

"Mr Rover, how about you come up to the front of the class? I need an answer to my question. How does poetry reflect life?"

"Yeah, sir... I mean Mr. Elijah."

I headed up to the front of the room. My thoughts were racing to all of my English classes in high school.

Poetry, life – what am I going to say? Where am I? This is one strange dream.

3

THE CATCH

Standing before the other private school students, I felt underprepared and exposed. Interestingly, I had on the uniform and even had stains from what must have been lunch on my trousers. So, I didn't *look* out of place, but I certainly felt out of my depth.

Mr. Elijah was sitting at his desk at the front of the classroom. He had this impish look that was a bit off-putting, but it had a calming effect on me too. Yet, there was an irritation behind his stare that made me dig into the depths of my knowledge of poetry.

"Go on Mr. Rover. Poetry. Life. What are your thoughts?"

I looked at the ceiling and even glanced at the Walt Whitman portrait on the wall for inspiration.

"Well, um, poetry gives us structure or boundaries on how things should unfold on a page. I guess poetry is like life, how we need structure to help us survive? I'm not a huge fan, but as a male artist, poetry helps me to fit what I'm doing with other creatives, and this is why we all go on to live differently to those who sat with us in school. I think there's more, but that might be where I stop."

I gulped and wished I had a water bottle; my throat was so dry.

"Can I go back to my desk?"

I looked around the room. All I saw was a bunch of blank stares. Then my eyes came back to the man behind the question. There he was, smiling.

"Well done, Mr Rover. But, where's the beauty, and is there more to poetry and life than merely a structured existence?"

At that moment, the bell rang for the end of class.

Every student grabbed his books and headed for the door. I was heading towards my desk when I felt a hand on my shoulder. I turned around. Mr. Elijah was looking into my eyes.

"Um, Mr. Rover, can you sit for a moment? Let's talk."

"Sure, I guess," I said.

None of the other students seemed to notice that I was being encouraged to stay behind. I could hear the boys running down the hall, heading to classes and dormitories. Instead of going to my desk, I sat in one of the seats closest to Mr Elijah's desk.

No one came into the classroom, and he sat on the front of his desk.

"Okay, Mr. Rover. You're not meant to be here, are you?"

All I could do was be honest.

"I'm not sure. The last thing I remember was riding my bicycle and a delivery truck. Then I was sitting in your class. I have no idea what I'm doing here."

He laughed with a jovial tone that made me nervous and comfortable. It was reminiscent of the teachers from all of the films that I had seen over the years.

"Well, son, you're here, and obviously, The Maker must need to get your attention."

The Maker? Did he mean God? This definitely went beyond the scripting of any film I was familiar with teachers as the focal point.

"Right," I said. "Not sure how to even respond to that. Who's The Maker?"

"Listen Cyrus, you hit the side of that delivery truck pretty hard," Mr. Elijah said, "and you're currently in a hospital bed in a coma."

He let that reality settle in, and his casual, modern tone surprised me.

I must have looked like a fish on a hook with my mouth wide open.

"Um, okay."

The teacher laughed again, then he sat down at the desk next to me.

"Cyrus, this is more than a dream. What you are experiencing is a spiritual connection with The Maker or, by another definition, God. He is trying to teach you something while you remain in hospital. Different people experience different things during these 'spiritual journeys.'"

He made the quotes sign with his fingers.

"What he has chosen to do is to tap into your love of film and utilize key characters from films to guide you through this time."

My expression didn't improve much. Now I was staring at the Walt Whitman picture with wide eyes. I wasn't even sure I had registered what the teacher was saying.

"Cyrus. Cyrus. Are you in there?"

He tapped me on the shoulder.

I shook my head and turned towards Elijah.

"Yeah, uh. Spiritual journey. Coma?"

"There we go, I've got your attention again," he smiled. "This is the beginning of something that can only be explained by God. Your accident left you in a time when He will be able to get your full attention. This is a journey that will surprise you, but those who will meet you along the way are there to help."

He paused to see if I heard him.

Suddenly, I was very aware of what was happening,

"'What? This is crazy! What do you mean, I'm in a coma? I'm supposed to learn something from movie characters? This is nuts. I love movies and I have some of my favorite genres, but this is next level. Come on, you're not real, right?'"

I stopped short, I wasn't sure how to handle this situation.

"Right. That's good to clarify," he said. "I'm the character within a genre of film that will connect with your soul. And I know, it all sounds crazy, but you're getting an opportunity that few get: direct communication from The Maker, and in a form you can connect with."

He took a breath.

"Movies."

"Cyrus, this is happening," he continued. "So, instead of freaking out, how about you embrace it?"

He put his hand on my shoulder and smiled at me like I was meant to accept the situation. All I could do was slump over and put my head on the desk. I needed to think. What was this? Why me? I was in a coma?

"Yeah, well, you don't have much time to consider this opportunity. Also, there is a bit of a catch."

He returned to leaning against his desk. My head shot up. I looked him in the eyes.

"Catch?"

"Well, yeah. Each lesson is meant to teach you something about life and The Maker. You can either take up the challenge or choose to ignore things. If you decide you aren't going to embrace the journey, well, you might not wake up. Sorry. Not to put the pressure on, but it is what it is."

He shrugged his shoulders and held his hands up in surrender. His words had definitely grabbed my attention.

"Well, I guess, I've no choice."

"No, you have a choice," he explained. "But it's cut and dried. One way or the other, and you need to make it quickly. Things are about to get started."

With that, he climbed up on the desktop and held out his hand.

"Oh captain, my captain?"

I shook my head and stood up. In disbelief, I reached out my hand. He pulled me up to my feet.

"Good choice. You're just about to start. I'll send you off to the next stage of the journey. Cyrus, are you ready?"

"I guess. Where..."

Suddenly, I was sitting in a large red leather wingback chair. The room was dark, and once my eyes adjusted to the lack of light, I could make out the outline of someone sitting across from me. His leather jacket, bald head, and signature glasses came into view.

It was Elijah, and he looks just like the Matrix mentor, Morpheus.

Discover the Third Space Discussion Guide that complements this chapter and join Cyrus Rover on his journey. You'll find the QR code to access them at the beginning of the book with the "Free Gift".

4

MEANWHILE BACK IN THE ICU

"His eyes are moving slowly, but the rest of his body isn't responding to any stimuli."

Sylvia was looking at the nurse on call.

"When Doctor Elisha comes back through, I'm sure he is going to say to keep the patient in the ICU. My only problem is that there's nothing keeping him in a coma besides a superficial blow to the head."

"All of his vitals look normal and, compared to other accidents, this doesn't make much sense why he is still... well, so still," She said, ticking off her patient's medical status.

Nurse Radka had worked in the ICU for the past five years and in the hospital for over 15 years. She had witnessed a great many trauma cases before leaving Bulgaria and immigrating to work in the Emergency Room. This kid was a bit of a mystery to her, too.

The intern kept looking at Cyrus' face.

"The other thing is his face looks unusually peaceful. Most coma patients can be mistaken for being dead, but their brain waves help us to know differently. This guy looks like he's still experiencing something. Can you see it, Raddy?"

"I guess?" the nurse admitted. "I'll get him cleaned up. His family has been waiting outside."

She waited to see if Sylvia was good with this before starting. The pair had connected over the years. Despite being in different parts of the staff, they had bonded through stressful work times. Also, they both had a faith that connected them after hours.

***

"Doctor, what's happening with my little Cy?"

Gramma Kat had a look of horror on her face as she stood by her grandson's bedside. Tears rolled down her face as she held his hand. Her gentleness spoke of a love that poured out of her soul and through the caresses of her fingers. She didn't look up from Cyrus, but there was no doubt that her tone said she needed answers.

Les Fremont stood on the other side of the room. He looked from his grandson to the medical staff and back again. His hands kept clenching and unclenching, like a man ready to head into the ring for a boxing match. No tears, but his nostrils flared like a raging bear holding back all of the emotions from someone harming her cub. He looked at Sylvia with an intensity that bore through to her heart. He cleared his throat, looked at the young intern, and then down at his wife who was sitting next to their grandson. He may have been older, but he didn't need to say much to say exactly what he wanted. The power behind his unrelenting stare said, "Answer my wife's question now."

Sylvia finally stopped looking with unexpected awe at this couple and looked down at the chart. She didn't need to look at the report, but it gave her a moment to gain her composure.

"Mrs. Fremont, do I have permission to call your grandson, Cyrus?"

Her request wasn't necessarily protocol. Still, it helped to break the tension and show respect at the same time. Then something unexpected happened. This emotional woman reached out and touched Sylvia's hand.

"Hon, you have our permission but know that we are on your side. We merely want to know what happened to our Cyrus. There isn't much we can do except pray. My husband and I need to know how to pray for you and him. So, take your time and tell us the truth. We love our grandson very much and want the best for him. Can you start by telling us your name?"

She gave the intern a gracious smile and then returned her attention to Cyrus.'

"My, my name is Doctor Sylvia Bloodworth. You can call me Doctor Sylvia, if that helps. Um, thank you for your prayers."

She cleared her throat and looked at the couple. Then she told them everything they knew about the accident, what procedures had been done, and Cyrus' current coma status.

"I wish we knew more, but we can say Cyrus is stable, and we are looking for answers to his situation. Any questions I can answer for you?"

With little warning, Les Fremont spoke up.

"Young lady, we're grateful. Please know that we will be prayin' for you. I want you to know that I'm not mad at you. It's just hard to see my grandson like this. Thank you for understanding."

Sylvia was taken aback at his speech, especially since Mrs. Rover seemed so articulate. What surprised her even more, though, was their willingness to express their faith. It was all a bit disarming.

"As a Christian, I appreciate the prayers. But, please know we all want the best for Cyrus. I will watch over him and hope he will break out of this coma soon."

"Thank you, darling," Gramma Kat said. "Can we have some time with our grandson? Just want to talk to him and pray."

Gramma Kat kept holding her grandson's hand with both of hers. Les sat down on the other side of the bed and put his hand on Cyrus' shoulder. Like a well-orchestrated moment, as if they had been doing this all their lives, the pair bowed their heads over the young man.

Sylvia wanted to stay and pray, but thought it would be better to leave the Fremonts alone for this time. She walked out and looked for the hallway bench. The young doctor was emotionally spent and sat for a minute. Then all she could do was take a moment to pray, too.

***

Lightning shattered the sky outside of the window behind the high wingback chair, enough that it startled the man sitting in the chair. That was when I noticed his face. It was , but now he was wearing cool shades and had on a long leather jacket.

"Hmm... there's a battle waging around us, Cyrus. Someone must be praying for you. Good."

"I guess," I said.

I recognized where I was, but things looked different than I expected. My clothes had changed. I looked into a mirror next to my chair. It was still my face, my body, after all. On top of it, I must have looked terrified – because I was. All I had were questions. What was going on? How did I get here? What did I need to do to get out of this?

Elijah looked back at me as if he could read my mind with his legs crossed and his fingers drumming on the arms of the chair. Suddenly, the cooler version of my guide seemed to settle back into the character of this scene. He stopped rapping his fingers on the chair and folded his hands in front of him. His index fingers and thumbs formed a triangle.

"Now, Cyrus, it's decision time."

Of course, I should have guessed. What was the decision I needed to make? Here we go.

5

THE DECISION

I sat there waiting for my film-traveling mentor to pull out the two pills for that moment of the decision. But, this cool, new version of Elijah just sat there, tapping his index fingers together.

"You must have so many questions, Cyrus."

"A few," I looked at him with a questioning and desperate look.

"You have five questions, then we must get you on your journey."

He barely moved, except for that slow tapping of his fingers.

"Oh. Okay. Five. Um, I guess the first would be, what the hell is going on?"

I surprised myself with the directness, but you have got to admit that this was bizarre and freaking me out. Genre jumping through iconic sequences and the best label I could think of on the spot was 'film travel.'

"I just left you in the setting of the teacher/student realm and now I'm in this dystopian scene that gets me excited and terrifies me at the same time. You have to help me understand what is happening. I'm kinda going out of my mind."

This at least got a small grin out of the man sitting across from me. He put his hand on the arms of the chair.

"As good a start as any," he smiled. "Cyrus, you're in what we call 'The Intermediate.' You were in an accident that caused your spirit to remain functioning while your body is in a state of dormancy. This is a unique time for you to be trained on how you should go forward in life. The Maker allows these things to happen so the person can learn something that will change their lives and change the world. You aren't going anywhere physically, but that doesn't mean you can't do something with your life. It's not a dream, this is really happening, but on more of a spiritual level. I explained this to you before, did you already forget?"

He gave me a sly grin.

"Yeah, no, I mean I remember, but it all came pretty fast," I said, sitting back in my chair. "You, I mean, the other you..."

I took a breath.

"Oh, man, this is getting weird," I sighed heavily. "Anyway, the previous 'you' did share part of this with me. Thanks for filling in some of the details. But, can you explain again why movie characters?"

"That's your second question, Mr. Rover," Elijah replied. "The Maker knows you better than you know yourself. He created you and put certain talents and gifts in place in your soul. He is creative and has given you a passion for the creative arts, specifically film. The Maker wanted to connect with you quickly and movies look to be the best path of communicating His message to you. This is a journey specifically designed for you. He has different paths for everyone he has created, but they are all meant to realize their purpose through this time. Does that make sense?"

This made me sit forward in my chair and rest my elbows on my knees.

"I think so. Wow. Purpose. Design. Journey. Sorry for my bluntness, since you act like I should know this already, but Mr Keating said The Maker was God, right? So, which one?"

'Ah, number three. Pretty critical," Elijah nodded. "He goes by different names, but Abba, YahWeh, Jehovah, Adonai or simply God are some of His names. For the sake of this journey, though, He is The Maker. He's the one you have been studying throughout your life. Pastor Hudson has done a good job in your life until now. The Maker is the name to stay with the theme of the creative process and being the One who made you and the whole journey of life you are on."

He smiled and sat back while he awaited my response.

My mouth was wide open. Stunned. Come on, I grew up in the church. Pastor Hudson was always investing his time in me and God was always at the heart of the conversation. My grandparents prayed, read their Bibles, and liked to talk with me about my faith. Still, I can't say I really believed in God. I know the stories about Jesus and the one about Adam and Eve, but The Maker? Hmmm...

"Right, I think I'm following you. Mind blown."

I flexed my hands next to my head with an expression of surprise added in for good measure.

"We might have a problem that could make this a very short trip. I'm not sure if I believe in God or The Maker. Does that make a difference?"

This got the leather-clad bespeckled man's attention.

"Good question. Number four," he said. "Just keeping a tab of your questions. The Maker knows everything, Cyrus. So, that's built into the journey. One thing He says is failure comes to those without guidance, but the person who has an abundance of counselors gains safe passage for the journey. You've had some great counselors in your life, but now The Maker is giving you mentors who will speak to you along this quest. Their words will guide you along the path, but right now you have to make a decision."

He paused and sat back and waited.

"You clever man, that leaves me with one question. Got it. I'll bite," I said. "What's my decision?'

I could only sit back with calm anticipation.

"Here is your decision Cyrus Rover," Elijah smiled. "Do you choose to take The Maker's Journey? I can't tell you anymore. I know you had a choice with Keating, but this is a stop-gap measure to make sure you know what you are getting into. Each step will get you closer to completion of this personal odyssey, but you must choose to go of your own free will. I can't force you. The Maker can't force you. If you decide to decline this invitation, you may awake in the hospital with no awareness of this opportunity. Honestly, I can't promise this, but you may awaken. Except there will be a constant niggling feeling of missing out on something that will always be there in your soul. Yet, on the other side, this choice does not guarantee your safety, but I can say it will change your life and the lives of all who you meet in the future. So, Cyrus Rover. What do you choose?"

"What? No red or blue pill?" I said, admittedly disappointed.

"Sorry, no more questions. But I can say, 'The way of a fool is right in his own eyes, but a wise man listens to advice.' My advice would be to take up The Maker's offer. But the decision is yours, Cyrus Rover."

Elijah sat there with his index fingers touching again. The light from the lamp in the corner seemed to shine through their triangular gap.

My heart was racing. My fingers were drumming on my knees. Was this a dream? Was this really happening to me? I could feel beads of sweat on my forehead and in the armpits of the business suit I was wearing.

"Okay," I said. "Well, it all seems a bit daunting and terrifying. But also tantalizing to the point that only a fool would say no. A journey without a safety net, except it has been designed by The Maker. Someone I'm not even sure I believe in. Right, got it. Morpheus, I think I will take your advice. I'll go."

I winced and waited for the silver goop to come out of the mirror and take me away.

"Wise choice, go well, Cyrus Rover.' He disappeared. I was alone and then I wasn't there anymore.

***

I suddenly found myself sitting in a chair before a fire. My clothes had changed to that of a well-dressed Englishman, except I was smaller. As I came out of my stupor, I could smell smoke. The sweet essence of a pipe. I looked around the room and behind a cloud of pipe smoke I could make out a familiar figure.

Yeah, it was Elijah, but not Elijah. He had transformed from the ominous figure in the wingback chair to a wizard with a long beard and robe to match.

Discover the Third Space Discussion Guide that complements this chapter and join Cyrus Rover on his journey. You'll find the QR code to access them at the beginning of the book with the "Free Gift".

6

PASTOR HUDSON AND THE LIFESAVING JOURNEY

"Hi, I'm sorry, I was looking for Cyrus Rover's room. Sorry to bother you. You do look busy."

The man before her was middle-aged and had a peaceful demeanor about him. He's got to be a minister of some sort, thought Sylvia.

"Doctor Bloodworth. You can call me Doctor Sylvia," she replied. "No hassle at all. Can I ask if you're family? Visiting hours are about to end."

She thought she knew the answer.

"Ah, thanks," he said, holding out his hand. "You have been on the prayer list at church. I hope that doesn't make you uncomfortable. Katy Fremont gave us your name. She talked very highly of you. Nice to meet the person we have been praying for. My name is Ray Hudson. I'm the pastor of the church that Cyrus attends when he's home. I have visitation credentials as pastoral care, but I'll try to stay out of the way. Just wanted to see Cyrus and pray for him. Could you direct me to his room?"

Sylvia shook his hand.

"I'm quite honored that you are praying for me," she admitted. "I've been praying for Cyrus, too. Strange case. He seems healthy enough, but he's not responding to anything yet. He is in room seven on the left. I can walk you there."

"Thank you, Doctor Sylvia. Are you a Christian?" he said without pausing as they walked to Cyrus' room.

"I am," Sylvia answered. "I never get to church as much as I'd like, though. Third-year intern. They keep me busy here."

They arrived at the room.

"This is it. I've got to finish my rounds," Sylvia said apologetically. "Thanks for the prayers. Have the nurses page me if you need anything."

"Thanks, Doctor", Pastor Hudson said, and headed into the room.

"Hey there Cyrus," he said. "Not sure if you can hear me, but it's me, Pastor Hudson. Your family and the church send their love. I was just going to pray for you. We are all hoping you recover quickly. God loves you, son."

The pastor pulled up a chair. He laid his Bible on the bed. Reached out, held Cyrus' arm, read to him for a time and then he started praying.

***

As my eyes adjusted to the light and pipe smoke, there was a crack of lightning outside the window. I hadn't noticed it was night, but the thunder and lightning were booming. The light shattered the sky like a beacon breaking through to capture my attention. Then as quickly as it had cracked outside the window, it stopped. No rain. Suddenly, it was daytime again. From where I was sitting, the landscape looked just like it did in many of my favorite fantasy films that included creatures like elves, dragons and wizards.

As the light broke through the front window, I was suddenly aware of my company. Elijah merely looked at me and puffed on his pipe as I got my bearings.

My brain was racing. Was I supposed to act like one of the creatures from this genre or could I just be myself? I wasn't sure what to do.

Suddenly, the familiar wizard put his pipe on the stand on the end table. He reached into his bag and pulled out a scroll.

"Well, well, Cyrus Rover. We've been waiting for you to arrive. I assume you got past the gatekeeper and now you are ready for instructions for the journey through the Intermediate."

"Um, yeah. I guess," I ventured. "Are you really a wizard? Are you meant to be..."

He held up his hand to forestall my question.

"Yes, I'm a wizard within this stage, but not the wizard you're thinking."

I was still a bit stunned by this whole experience. It was daunting to be sitting across from a realistic sorcerer garbed in a hat and robe. I could see a wand on the table next to his chair.

"Son, I'm the representation of a wizard and I am meant to guide you through the next steps. Are you hungry?"

He pointed at a table to the left of his chair. There were a selection of foods, from bread to cheese and shaved meats. Honestly, I hadn't even thought about it. Yet, I was surprised to find I was hungry.

"Yeah, thanks. Can we eat? You can keep talking and explaining things to me," I said, feeling a bit awkward. "Will you eat with me?"

I approached the table.

"Of course," Elijah said, laughing that familiar chuckle. "I've been waiting for you to come around. Food is a wonderful way to get to know someone. Also, I think you will need some sustenance as we work through your journey."

He grabbed the scroll as he joined me at the table. We prepared our plates, he poured some wine and we settled down to a deep discussion.

"Cyrus, this is an incredibly special opportunity from The Maker. You've only to step out in faith to go forward with this journey. It can take as long as you need, but the longer you take, the longer your body will remain in the state it's in at the hospital. How about I tell you the steps of your journey and the ultimate quest? Then I will explain the 'cost' of things."

He made the quote symbol with his fingers when he said cost. I stopped eating and sat back.

"Wait, wait. Cost? What cost? No one said anything about a cost."

The wise man shook his head and sipped his wine.

"Ah, you want to know the cost upfront. Fair," he said, sitting back with his glass and looked me directly in the eye. "Cyrus, you should know everything has a cost. No such thing as a free lunch and all that. This journey is going to cost you. Specifically, you will be given supplies for the journey, but each excursion stage will have a cost. You'll have to make choices on what you are willing to sacrifice. Some sacrifices will be harder than others, but each decision will cost you. Also, you'll have to complete the journey to return to life outside of this realm. This quest will test the very essence of your soul. My son, the cost isn't really defined now, but you must know it will cost you."

He stopped, took a bite of the meat on his plate, and then had another sip of wine.

'Still...' he paused.

It was one of those painfully long pauses that cause your heart to cave in before it ends.

"Cyrus, hear me now. This journey will reward you beyond measure if you can see it through to the end."

Suddenly I wasn't as hungry as I'd been before.

"I think I follow you," I said. "How about you fill me in on this 'quest.' I don't have to take a ring to a volcano, right?"

This got a belly laugh from the old wizard.

"Bah, no, that's been done," he smiled. "No, this quest has been made just for you, young man. Let me explain."

He stood and moved our plates to the side. Then he unrolled the scroll before me. It was a map of an unfamiliar land. At the top it said, *Fay Enaid* and there looked to be a border around the edges. It was unlike anything I remembered my high school world history teacher describing but, honestly, I only just passed that class. The main thing I could see on the map was a large dot and the word, Dechrau.

"The Maker has designed this map for you, Cyrus," Elijah said. "This dot represents the beginning of your journey. Once you complete the next task, the following part of your trip will appear on the map. Each person has a different number of destinations within their quest. The land you find in yourself is *Fay Enaid* which simply represents your soul. The community you are in currently is

Dechrau since all journeys must have a beginning. I can't tell you what is next, but once you head out this door, the next stop on your map will appear. I apologize, you will not know how many stops you must experience, but when you get close, your guides will share their knowledge of the next portion of the journey."

Elijah went over to his pipe. He tapped it on the edge of the fireplace. Then he stoked the fire a bit, filled his pipe, and lit it with a stick drawn from the flames. Meanwhile, I studied the map. There wasn't much to see, except what the wizard had pointed out. Yet, there was something magical about the piece of paper. It seemed to be, I don't know, *living*. Nothing could explain it, but the map almost seemed to be breathing and it had an energy that seemed to electrify my hand when I touched it. The pulse resonated through my body like nothing I'd ever experienced before.

"Now, I will help you by preparing your bag," the wizard said. "There are certain items you will need for your journey. They are yours and you may choose to trade them along the way. Yet, be wise with each of these provisions. They serve a purpose and cannot be replaced."

He stopped to make sure I was listening. I looked at him, then the map, and back at this towering man.

"I'm listening, I promise. You've got all my attention. Especially after that 'cost speech," I admitted. "Whoa, a lot to process."

Elijah took a few more puffs on his pipe, then looked me over a bit.

"Right, there are some essentials you are going to need, but other items you will need to get on the way. Packing light will be important, but let's get some key things into your bag."

He sighed momentarily and then grabbed the bag off the table.

"First is this multipurpose tool, we will call it a sigil," he said.

It looked like the one of those multi-tools my grandfather always had on his belt. He always called it a Swiss Army knife, but this one had a beautiful, antiqued look.

"This is small but vital for your journey. It has all of the normal items you need but with a few adjustments. You can use some of the knives as weapons and others provide their own wise counsel along the way."

He pulled out a hooded jacket that looked like those fold-up windbreakers you get at rock concerts before a rain shower.

"Now this looks rather thin, but it is magical. This will protect you from all inclement weather, but if something evil wants to harm you, it hardens like metal and even has a glow if danger is around you."

"Wow, not sure I want to see that work, because of the evil bit," I said, confused but also a bit excited. "Still, sounds cool."

"This belt not only will hold the multipurpose tool, but it gives you discernment if someone you are with is lying to you," Elijah continued. "Here, put it on."

I obliged and it fit like it was made for me.

"Cyrus, let's test it out. Your eyes are purple."

It was an obvious lie. At that moment the belt seemed to vibrate a bit. Not weirdly. I could feel it tingle?

"That is strange, but I guess it will help."

I adjusted it a bit and then slid the tool on. Then Elijah pulled out a wide-brimmed hat that seemed ideal for hiking.

"This hat can harden if things get dangerous, while still being foldable enough to be put in your bag. It will protect you from the elements and will keep your head warm. If you believe in it's magic, you can't lose it. This hat is like a boomerang, it will always return to you, even if you try to reject it."

"Okay, Elijah. The bag is looking pretty full. Do I need more? How about some food?"

I reached out for the bag, but he slowly pulled it back to himself.

"Almost done, my friend. Here are some boots that will always keep your feet dry, warm, and surprisingly fresh for walking – always ready for the next stage! But, something to remember, the bag will always feel perfectly balanced, unless you try to add unnecessary things to it. And..." he said, stretching the word, "if you put it in front of your chest, it can also be a shield to protect you."

With that, he handed the shoes and bag to me.

"Now put them all on, and I'll pack some food in the bag. Then you're ready."

The boots felt great. As I was putting them on, I could see the wizard putting food carefully into the bag. As I put the bag on my back and the hat on my head, I smiled and looked up at the man.

"Now what?"

At that instant, the lightning cracked outside, and I heard a knock on the door.

7

THE CHICAGO WAY OF JUSTICE

As I answered the door, I felt a gentle push through it, and suddenly I found myself standing on a dark city street. I turned around to look back into the house, but the building behind me looked like one of the homes on the streets of the 1930s films I had grown up watching with my grandparents. The air smelt of recently fallen rain, and the industrial scent of local trains mixed with a whiff of a cologne that reminded me of my grandfather's aftershave. That is when I felt a firm hand on my shoulder, and I turned to look into the eyes of a police officer from what looked like the 1920s. The clothes and buildings around me were all reminiscent of the gangster films of the Depression era. I knew it was Elijah, but he looked weathered and older as he smiled and then shook my hand.

"Hey there, boyo. Been waitin' for yas."

He even had a soft Irish accent that made it all authentic and helped my head to adjust to the changes.

I looked down at his hand, shaking mine, and noticed that my clothes had changed to fit the era. My satchel had become something that looked like an overnight leather bag. I reached up, grabbed my hat, and noticed it had become one of those cool fedoras of the era. My shoes were now finely polished wingtips, while the belt was stylish under a waistcoat that had once been my jacket. Yet, Sigil was still hooked to the belt, and it had not changed even though it was covered by my finely tailored suit coat. I must have looked a bit perplexed as I looked back up at the beat cop from this genre.

Elijah laughed in an Irish manner that was convincing but required an adjustment to understand.

"You look likes you could use some food and a drink, Cy. Let's get you to the pub and I'll get you familiar with what is happening here."

He pulled me along down what I assumed was a street in Chicago, and we headed straight to a bar with a neon light shaped like a shamrock in the window. Could this get any more cliche?

Elijah ordered me a Reuben sandwich and a pint of beer as we walked to a booth in the back corner. There weren't too many issues with 18-year-olds drinking on that day and this must have been post-Prohibition. I slid into the seat and set my bag down near to the wall. He sat across from me and we both set our hats on the table. Within seconds, two pints of Guinness were in front of us and he smiled at me.

"So son, you've walked through the door. And what are you prepared to do now that you're in Chicago?"

Almost on cue, the sandwich showed up at the table and I found I was surprisingly hungry, it smelled so good. As I picked up half of the sandwich, I looked him in the eye with unexpected confidence.

"Actually, I was pushed," I said, "and now I'm waiting for you to answer that question. Want part of the sandwich?"

He laughed again.

"Naw, Guinness is right for me."

He took a drink, wiped off his lips.

"Yeah, now I'm meant to prepare you for what is next. But, can I ask ya somethin'?"

"Sure," I said with my mouth full of the delicious Reuben.

"Good. Are you prepared to go all the way? You must be prepared to go all the way. You can't go back and you've gotta be committed my friend. The Chicago way will get you through the next few parts of the journey. But you need to know that you will face different types of opposition and each stage of this journey is meant to teach you something about yourself and God. What are you prepared to do?"

He stopped and looked at me with expectation and obviously an answer. With apprehension in my voice and little confidence in this whole sequence of events, I answered.

"I guess I'm willing to do whatever I need to do."

A fire suddenly came into his eyes.

"You guess? You guess? Well, that's not going to do, son. That won't do at all."

Angry, he seemed to spit the words through his teeth in his newly found Irish accent.

"You ain't surviving this trip if you guess."

"Okay, okay. I'm willing to do whatever it takes," I said. "But are you telling me I won't wake up unless I get through this? Come on, what's going on?"

Now I was terrified. All the other experiences were odd and disorienting, but this one scared me to my soul. But he smiled considerately and then slid two things across the table to me. A revolver and a set of handcuffs.

"Cy, you've got to finish this thing. Each stage is meant to teach you something about how you are meant to live for The Maker. An attribute in each scenario. How you respond will determine if you learned the lesson and are prepared to head onto the next stage. Got it?"

"Yeah, but honestly this is all a bit bizarre."

As I took another bite of the sandwich I realized I wasn't hungry anymore.

"If that's the case, what should I learn from you?" I asked. "From this scene or stage or whatever you want to call it."

I took a swig of Guinness. It was surprisingly cool and refreshing.

"Now, you're asking the right questions. Put the pistol and the cuffs on your seat," he said, looking around the room and then leaning in. "Justice. You are meant to learn about justice. How do you respond to injustice, and what justice really means."

Suddenly a thin, angular man with prominent features that were even more pronounced in his wide-lapeled suit walked up to the side of the booth. His face was reminiscent of a weasel, and he seemed to be smiling out of the side of his mouth.

"Apollyon, Frank Apollyon. What...?" the Irish Elijah said angrily.

The man in the finely tailored suit moved in quick as a flash and lunged at the police officer and then at me. I felt a pressure against my vest and heard something that sounded like steel breaking. Then the man ran to the back of the shop to what looked like an exit.

I looked down and a knife was broken in two on the seat next to me. My waistcoat seemed to be glowing, and I remembered what the wizard version of Elijah had said about it hardening like metal and glowing when danger was around. Then I quickly looked across the booth and saw my new friend leaning against the wall with his hand on his side. Blood was spilling out between his fingers. He had been stabbed. I started to yell for help.

"Someone call an ambulance!"

"CY! CY!" I heard Elijah saying through labored breaths. "Cy! What are you prepared to do? Get Apollyon. Don't let him get away."

I didn't think, I didn't know what I was doing, but something instinctive happened. I grabbed the gun, the cuffs, and my bag and started running towards the back door where Apollyon had exited. As I went through, I realized this wasn't an exit so much as a set of stairs. They only went up, and I could hear someone running up to the roof. It had to be at least five or six flights. Then I suddenly felt myself pursuing him, this wasn't my natural instinct. This seemed to be my character wanting to pursue the criminal.

As I made it to the door to the roof, I charged through and a bullet grazed off of my hat. This caused me to dive behind a column of chimneys. I remembered my gun and set my bag by the brick wall behind me. I felt my head. The hat seemed hard as a rock and there was no blood.

"Hey copper," the gangster called. "That was supposed to be a message for you both. The cop downstairs and you's was supposed to understand to stop pursuing my boss. You's understand?"

I didn't know what to say. I remembered the film's storyline, and my situation was reminiscent of the scene where Elliot Ness threw the assassin off the building. It was his own brand of justice, but was this what I was supposed to do?

"Um, Mr Apollyon – how about we talk this over?"

"Mr Apollyon? Mr Apollyon?" he replied. "Wat's you asking? No talk. I'm walking out of here. If you's gets in my way, yous dead. Got it, copper?"

I could hear fear masked by vibrato in his voice. As he was talking I managed to sneak around behind him and could see him on the other side of the wall. He was near the edge of the building's roof. What was I to do? I hadn't shot a gun in my life.

"Your friend was as easy to stick as a stuck pig. Deserved it. Pig copper," Apollyon was saying. "If you don't let me go, you will be bleeding soon, too."

He moved closer to the edge looking down, as if looking for an escape. I was close enough to run at him and push him over the edge. Gun? Push? What was I supposed to do? Justice? Ugh, this was impossible. Then I remembered something Elijah had said in the fantasy realm.

I grabbed a loose pipe that was on the roof and threw it away from me and across from Apollyon. The hitman stood up and shot his pistol towards the clang of the pipe. Then I threw my hat at him, not knowing if it would work, but it hit its mark. As it hit him in the head, the man fell over. Surprisingly, the hat flew straight back to me, just like Elijah had said it would. It was undamaged. As I slipped it back on, I stayed close to the wall and moved close to where Apollyon had been. As I rounded the corner, I pointed my gun at him, even though I didn't know if I could have used it. There he was, knocked out on the ground. I kept my gun pointed at him and kicked him. I could hear a moan and saw a dark red mark on his head. Quickly, I got out the handcuffs and put them on him while he lay on the ground. Almost instantly, two police officers came charging through the door with their guns in hand.

"Detective, where are you?" they yelled.

I guess that's who I was a police officer from this era, doling out my own form of justice. I raised my hands.

"Over here," I said, standing up.

They came over and roughly picked up Apollyon.

"We've got him," the younger of the two officers said. "Your partner's been taken to the hospital, he should be okay. Tough old bastard."

We headed toward the door. They took Apollyon through first and then I followed suit after I grabbed my bag. As I closed the door, I suddenly found myself in a basement smelling like a nasty combination of sweat, blood, and urine. My 1930s suit had turned into a modern business suit and my hat seemed to have turned into rose-colored sunglasses. I had on a creased white shirt, my vest was rumpled and had some blood on it. My bag had turned into a backpack, and I looked across the dark room and could make out a figure with a cigarette dangling off his lip. Covered in sweat and shirtless, there stood a man ready for a fight.

As lightning struck outside the window of this warehouse, I heard a call to action. The voice was familiar.

"Gentlemen, tonight we fight to the end."

It was Elijah, but he looked tough as nails and even had a black eye.

Discover the Third Space Discussion Guide that complements this chapter and join Cyrus Rover on his journey. You'll find the QR code to access them at the beginning of the book with the "Free Gift".

8

FIGHTING FOR MY LIFE

"Lord, I pray my boy fights for 'is life. I'm not givin' up on 'im. I know you aren't givin' up on my Cyrus. Please 'ear my prayers, Lords Jesus."

Grandpa Les was in the hospital room on his own. Even though Gram Katy wasn't able to travel to the hospital, her husband didn't miss a day at the bedside of their grandson. Even though he struggled to keep up with the boy when he was younger, the grandfather deeply loved Cyrus.

Radka had walked in while the elderly man was praying for his grandson. She was fascinated with the perseverance of this man. His devotion was inspiring despite being a quiet, simple man. He was always polite, greeted the staff with a smile, and was willing to chat at the main desk.

"Oh hello, Nurse Radka," Les said. "Lovely to see yas. How's my boy? Is he behaving himself?" He said with a wink.

He gave his attention to the nurse but continued to hold Cyrus' hand. She walked in and smiled at Les.

"We've had to keep an eye on Cyrus. He can be a handful," she laughed. "Actually, I need to do his vitals. You can stay in the room if you like."

"Thanks, but I need to get back to my Katy," Les said. "She wishes she could've come, but busy day today. Take care of our Cy. I'll talk to him tomorrow about 'is behavior.'

He gave her another wink and patted his grandson's hand.

"Loves you, my boy. Hope to see your eyes open tomorrow. Take care, hon," he said, getting up and waving at Radka. "See you tomorrow."

Then he headed out the door in the direction of the elevators.

Radka got to caring for her patient but couldn't stop thinking about Les' devotion for his grandson. She wondered what she would do if her son was the one lying here? As she checked Cyrus' pulse, the experienced nurse could see his other hand making a fist like he was ready to punch someone.

***

There was a lightning strike outside. The room lit up for a second as I heard Elijah going on with the rules for the action that was happening all around him.

When he had finished, two guys came out from the shadows into the centre of the room. My eyes were still adjusting to the light as I moved through the crowd. The place smelled of men, sweat, and body odor. It all seemed to mix into the dust and what I could only imagine was blood on the floor. The two guys smiled at one another and then the bigger man hauled off and slapped the other across the face. The room erupted with cheers as the two men boxed, wrestled and punched one another.

Looking on with fascination and horror, I suddenly noticed Elijah walking toward me.

"Cyrus, Cyrus. Welcome to this portion of your journey," he said. "Hmm, you'd think that this is the most brutal chapter, but I can't promise you that. At least it will toughen you up for the rest of your quest."

He flicked his cigarette into the dark and the sparks flew as it hit what I assumed was the floor. I was surprised. Should a guy who works for The Maker be smoking? But it did fit the character, and I don't think there are any Bible passages about cigarettes. If I got a chance, I'd ask Pastor Hudson about it.

"Guess you needed to see some real action as opposed to some softer guys they send people to."

He talked with a tone that was unlike any of the other versions of himself. This Elijah was rough and scary. My brain clicked in. This whole thing was connected. What was happening? Why would The Maker use this nasty version of Elijah as part of his plan for me to learn something? I'll admit, I thought the film it was referencing was brilliant and David Fincher is one of my favorite directors. Still, I'm not sure I was going to like this chapter. I smiled nervously as I watched the two men pummel each other and the crowd around them seemed to be working themselves into a frenzy.

"Right, you did choose correctly, since you're here," Elijah said. "Well, grab your little bag there. Nice hat by the way, but I'm more of a Jets fan."

He turned around and went to the corner of the room with a table set up. I pulled off my hat. Detroit Lions was written across the front. Bizarre. I hate football; I'm more of a baseball guy. Detroit? What was that about? I put it back on and nothing was glowing, which means no danger I reminded myself. Even in this room of bloody brutality. Something crunched under my foot. I looked down. It was someone's tooth. I looked over at the fight and they were pulling the bigger guy off the floor. He was bleeding from his mouth and from a gash in his forehead. Yet, he was smiling. Missing one tooth, sure, but there was an unmistakable grin on his face.

"Yo, Cyrus. You comin'?"

Elijah had on a vintage Hawaiian shirt and red jacket. His hair was even perfectly shaped. How did he do that?

"We're meeting Barney at the group session. Focus."

He headed towards a set of stairs with a dim light above them. I ran after him as the next fight started. I thought, who's Barney?

We walked down a city street that looked like so many movie sets that could have been shot in Delaware or Vancouver. At least it looked like the right set for the familiar storyline. Elijah walked a few steps ahead of me and was smoking another cigarette. Then he suddenly jumped up a set of stairs and headed into a building with a 'Community Center' sign over the door. The 'er' had fallen off the sign at some point, so that it read 'Community Cent'. It described the room well. There was a pungent odor that wasn't much better than the warehouse we had just come from. The room must have been an old basketball court at some time. Maybe that was the smell. The hoops were still up on the walls, but the floor had chairs strewn across it and the space didn't look like it had been used for sports in a while. The smell was a mixture of cigarettes, human despair, body spray trying to mask poor hygiene, and old wood that reminded me of the gym back home at my elementary school.

In the center of the room was a circle of chairs with people talking. One guy who stood out was a massive man who could have been the Barney that Elijah mentioned. He looked like a former bodybuilder who had let himself go. The man was huge and had a powerful air about him except for his huge gut and the man boobs that tend to form on guys who have steroids in their past. It was hard to miss him, and he cried as he shared his story with the group. The people sitting next to him were consoling the monster of a man. Elijah remained quiet and stood in the shadows smoking.

"Cyrus, I never needed these groups," he said, leaning over to me, "but Barn seems to get so much out of them. We will get you on your journey once he's done getting in touch with his emotions. Hungry? There are donuts in the corner. Pretty good ones, too."

"Thanks, Elijah."

I looked at him, the group and then the donuts in the corner.

"Look, you can be all nice, but it ain't really necessary," he laughed. "Since you're here, it means we've got to toughen you up for the journey. You can call me whatever you want. But know this, Cyrus, this is going to hurt a bit."

He smiled and then took another pull on his cigarette. Smoke came out his nose. His character even made smoking look cool. But my head was screaming, 'What?' My stomach was growling, too. I hadn't had much of the sandwich in Chicago. I was hungry, but my mind was spinning. I must have looked like I was going to faint when I felt a huge hand on my shoulder.

"Eli, he looks like he's about to piss his pants."

It was Barney, standing over me and laughing.

"You aren't meant to scare him to death you idiot," he said, looking me up and down. "You must be the new kid. I'm Barney or you can call me Barnabus if you like. Calm down, it isn't going to be that bad. Take a breath. Grab a couple of donuts and then we'll go to the house. Nice hat. I'm more of a Dolphins fan myself."

He drew me to him, hugged me and buried me in his man boobs. It was unsettling but comforting at the same time.

"Thanks," I said, pushing him away. "Yeah, I'm hungry. Be right back. Um, nice to meet you?"

He laughed as I walked over to the table. The group had broken up and there were only a few donuts left. It didn't really matter, I just grabbed a white one and a pink-coated donut. I didn't like the fake strawberry-flavored one, but I was hungry. I returned to the mismatched pair with a donut in my mouth, crumbs on my jacket, and we headed out of the building.

***

We walked across town. Barney and Elijah talked while they hit car lights out with baseball bats. I didn't even see where those came from, but they seemed to enjoy it, especially the VW Beetles. Then we headed down this rundown street towards what looked like an abandoned house. The guys looked back at me and laughed. Elijah went inside and I started to walk up the stairs towards the door when Barney stopped me.

"Nah, Cyrus, right? You need to wait out here. We'll tell you when you can come in – " he paused – "*if* you can come in. Stand there," the big man smiled, pointing to a veranda on the porch by the door. It was exposed to the elements, but close to the entrance.

What was going on? I couldn't figure this part out. One stage I was making choices, the next had me being equipped for the journey and the last phase was there to help me determine my sense of justice. What was this? Why this nasty version of Elijah? He was the epitome of cool, but this didn't seem like the place to learn something about God.

Suddenly the door banged open. Elijah came charging out and punched me in the stomach. He didn't hold back, this was no dream, it hurt like being hit with a baseball bat. As I doubled over in pain from the punch, he leaned down.

"You're done. Do you think God is with you?" he whispered in my ear. "Leave."

I was holding my stomach but caught my breath before he headed inside the house.

"What?" I gasped. "You've gotta be kidding me."

He turned around, lighting another cigarette.

"Wait around, I don't care. Whatever. You're done," he said, slamming the door behind him.

Now what was I gonna do?

9

INITIATION

"It's not regular, but seeing muscle spasms in coma patients isn't abnormal."

Radka was on for the night shift and had contacted Sylvia since she was on call. The pair were talking about their young patient.

"Honestly, I haven't had many coma patients, but I had noticed Cyrus twitches occasionally," the intern said, looking at his chart. "After studying up on it again, I remembered every case can be different. Still, his spasms always seem to be localized. The other day, he was clenching his hand. While today it's almost like he is being hit in the stomach. Strange."

Radka was checking Cyrus' vitals. She heard Sylvia's words, but she felt a connection with the young man. She couldn't shake it. Whenever the nurse was in his room, she felt an odd feeling. Even though she had believed in the spiritual realm throughout her life, she hadn't ever felt it before. Some churches had these rituals that addressed the spirit stuff, but this wasn't normal for her. So, this was all new, but she felt something each time she came into Cyrus' room.

"Raddy, did you hear me?"

As the nurse turned, she saw Sylvia looking at her worriedly.

"Oh, sorry. I was lost in my thoughts," she said, facing the intern and giving the woman her full attention. "What did ya say?"

"Cyrus doesn't need anything extra," she said, repeating herself. "But we might want to regularly rotate him. Bed sores, you know. Are you okay?"

'Yeah, we have that on his schedule," Radka replied. "Normal protocol for coma patients. And, um, I'm not sure you will get what's going on with me."

The nurse looked at the intern to see her response.

Without hesitating, Sylvia sat down in the chair in the corner.

"Try me. If you share, I'll give you something too," she smiled, and a sip from her water bottle.

"Right. Well, I've really got to get to my other patients – it's a crazy weekend. But..."

The nurse leaned against the window sill.

"I just get a strange vibe about Cyrus. You might get it, you're Christian. Yeah, whenever I come into this room, there's, well, a spiritual feeling I can't shake.'

She paused to see what expression Sylvia was giving her.

Suddenly the young doctor leaned forward.

"Like a battle, or something? Right?"

"What? You feel it too?" Radka said, surprised.

"Yeah, every time I call on Cyrus. He twitches or something. He seems to be in some sort of fight. His physical body has healed. I can only chalk it up to some sort of spiritual battle," Sylvia explained. "I can't put in the report, but this boy is going through something pret intense. Not sure how I know, but there's something that tells me that he's fighting for something."

She took another sip of her water bottle, contemplatively.

Radka relaxed.

"I thought it was only me," she said. "I know that all I can do is pray, but he is going through something on a different level, I think. Spiritual, maybe."

The nurse stood up, realizing she needed to get on with her rounds.

"Hey Raddy, could we pray for him together?" Sylvia asked. "We don't have to tell anyone. But, well, um, I think it would make me feel like I was doing, I don't know, something for him."

The intern stood up with a hopeful look in her eyes.

The nurse looked over at Cyrus.

"Yeah. Let's do it."

Each of the women stood over the film student and prayed.

***

Lightning struck at that moment and showed light over my confusion.

I was doubled over on the front porch of the house. Elijah had walked back in after lighting his cigarette. He didn't say anything else.

My brain was working through everything. I leaned back against the painted-chipped wooden railing and just sat there for a bit. I still had my bag, I looked down at my rumbled clothes. I must have looked as disheveled as some of the guys in the shed who were fighting. I couldn't understand why the shirt didn't protect me and nothing in this strange set of equipment gave me any warning. No shining. No vibrating. Nothing. At that moment, Barney walked out. He reached down with those massive hands and lifted me up. Then he started to dust me off and straightened my jacket. He kicked my bag a bit closer to me.

"Cyrus, listen to me," he said. "This journey is not meant to be easy. This stage is meant to toughen you up. Also, it is meant for you to realize what tools you have in that fancy bag. Elijah and I are immune to anything that would protect you from pain. We're here to serve a purpose. But what's crazy, we're here to help. Still, it's gonna hurt a bit, little man."

He let out a big sigh, then looked me in the eye.

"This stage of the journey is meant to remind you what you have in that bag. While you sit out here in the cold, take some time to look through that bag. Check out the map, be sure to remember what's in it. Now how do ya want your pain?"

He was dead serious.

"What? Barn, what's going on?"

"Cy, I don't have any more time," Barnabus replied. "You're gonna need to stand out here and prove your resolve. Listen to my advice. Look through the bag. Now, choose your pain. Stomach, face or legs?"

I could tell he was serious.

"Okay. I think I remember this. This is the initiation, right? Bag, got it. Pain, um, leg?"

I grimace at the anticipation of what was to come. Suddenly, I felt his foot sweep me off my feet, and Barney kicked me in the thigh while I was laying on the porch. I screamed.

"Argh, oh my God!"

At that moment, the mountain of a man screamed in my face as I laid on the ground.

"Quit! Stop! God doesn't want you! Leave! We don't want you!"

Then he got down close to my ear.

"Bag. Map. Fight for this, Cy, fight for this."

With that he headed back in the house.

After some time I stopped feeling the pain in my leg and got myself up against the railing again. This time I reached into my bag to see what was in there. Everything felt different than it did when Elijah the wizard had packed it, but every piece felt familiar.

First thing was that the title *Fay Enaid* was missing. The scroll had turned into a map that said Delaware on the front cover. I unfolded it and that is when it started to look familiar. It was like the scroll the wizard had rolled out before me but now had different lines and dots on it. They didn't represent cities, but people. There was the wizard, the beat-cop, and now the ruffian. Interesting, there was a dotted line coming off the dot from the ruffian. In the corner of the map was a legend, it hadn't been there before. Inside the box, there were words. 'Wisdom' and 'justice' were as clear as day, but I could see other words forming. They weren't clear, but it looked like 'perseverance' and 'courage', but it was hard to read in the light from the street lamp. Another thing was a large star forming in the map's corner. I wasn't sure what that was, but it was fascinating to see this map form before my eyes.

After I folded it up, I reached in to see what was in the bag. There was Sigil. It looked like a multi-tool and I reattached it to my belt. In this scenario, the belt looked more like a dress belt.

"I understand what's going on right now," I whispered. "The belt is vibrating. It still works."

There was another bolt of lightning and this time a thunderclap followed. Then it started bucketing rain. This made me reach into the bag to find the jacket. Now it looked like a hooded trench coat. I pulled it on just in time. I felt warm and didn't even notice the rain that was blowing under the ricke porch roof. I remembered the shoes, which now looked like black work boots. Still, I was warm, dry and feeling better about this scenario. As I stood in the rain, water dripping off my hat, I felt pretty good. My leg still hurt a bit, but I was warm, dry, and firm.

At that moment the door opened, Elijah was standing there.

"Kid, are you ready to quit? The rain ain't stoppin'. You ain't comin' in. Time to quit. The Maker doesn't want you."

Instead of responding with questions or attitude, I just stood there. Looked straight ahead.

"Didn't you hear me, fool? You're done. You need to wonder if God wants you. Quit. Leave."

He slapped me across the face and then flicked a cigarette over the verandah railing of the steps.

I snapped back into position and stood there. Even though my cheek was aching like a sonofabitch, I wasn't leaving. My eyes kept looking ahead.

"Oh, you'll quit," he laughed. "Don't worry. You'll quit."

The door slammed shut.

I stood as the rain came down, but there seemed to be something forming in me that I didn't know was there before. Strength I never knew I had until now. At that moment, a lightning bolt shot across the sky and was complemented by a rumble of thunder.

***

Radka and Sylvia quit praying and both started to head out to the hallway. Neither noticed that Cyrus was lying there with hands clenched tight. Yet, his body seemed to convey a peacefulness that hadn't been there earlier.

10

THE FIGHT FOR THE JOURNEY

I wasn't sure how long I was out there. Things always seemed gray around me. It rained, the wind blew, I found some food in my bag that Elijah had put in there, but the old verandah under the leaking roof. This version of my guide and Barney would come out and tell me to quit, push me, yell at me, and then go back in. Then something changed. The weather turned sunnier, the rain stopped, and the berating stopped too.

Barney walked out in the morning light and handed me a cup of coffee in an old mug.

"Well, you made it. Didn't think you'd had it in ya, Cy. Grab your bag. Come inside."

He turned around and started to head toward the door. I set the coffee on the porch railing, reached out and grabbed him.

"What? Come on, Barn. What gives? That's all I had to do? Stand here?"

He turned around and without warning he yelled.

"CYRUS! It is not your time to ask 'why.' You've moved through the grace period. Everything will be explained inside, but don't have me ask ya again. Got it?"

He wrenched his massive arm from my grip and entered the house, leaving the door open. Stunned, I did what I was told. I picked up my bag and headed in. Inside the door was a guy with a towel, soap, and razor. He handed them to me. I never saw anyone come into the house except Elijah and Barnie. Who was this guy? He gave me some direction.

"Listen to me. Bathroom and shower is over there," he said, pointing towards a small room that hadn't been cleaned in years. "Clean up and get back out here. You don't have much time. Things are happening and we are about to head off."

I looked at him and the towel and then back up at him.

"Now!" he yelled at me. "Why are you lookin' at me, idiot? Get cleaned up and get back out here."

He shoved the things into my arm that wasn't holding my bag. As he walked away, they fell to the floor.

I'd been standing outside so long, it took me a minute to move. I finally picked up the toiletries and went to the bathroom. The room was so disgusting that it was an incentive to get out of there as fast as I could. Even though the shower felt good and taking a leak in a toilet did feel more civilized, this bathroom was gross. Sure, there was a small toothbrush in the towel and I brushed my teeth. As I got dressed, I may have been wearing the same clothes I arrived in, but now I felt clean. Actually, I felt like a new man.

I threw everything into my bag and headed out to the main room. To my surprise the room was packed with most of the guys from the fight club. They were all dressed in black and each of them looked ahead in an uneasy military formation. So, I walked by them and didn't look anyone in the eye except when I saw Elijah and Barney at the front of the room.

"Cyrus, come on up here."

Elijah was in his signature shirt and Barney looked pret serious.

"Kid, I honestly didn't think you had it in you, but you made it," he smiled, lighting a cigarette. "You got through the next step on your journey. But, now get ready for the pain."

I shook my head in disbelief.

"What? More pain?"

"SHUT UP! Listen to me," he yelled. "We're here to help you get through this next section of the journey. This is for your own good. Give me your map."

Then, unexpectedly, he looked genuinely helpful.

I grabbed my bag, but then unzipped it. As I reached in and grabbed the map.

"Elijah, what's going on?" I said, handing him the map.

"Alright Cy, listen," he said, unfolding the map on the table behind him. "If you want to survive the night and get out of here, you need to listen. See this path on your nif little map?"

I looked down and there was a path that hadn't been there before. It went down two blocks east and three blocks south.

"Yeah, I see it. What's it mean?"

"Look at it, memorize it," he sighed. "Remember the name 'Spunk Cafe.' That is where this gets you to. But you are gonna have to fight to get there. Run, fight, keep runnin' some more. You got it memorized?'

He looked at me with an intensi that cut through me and kept my full attention.

"Yeah, yeah. Two blocks east and three blocks south. Spunk Cafe. Run. Fight. Run. What do you mean?"

He handed me the map and I put it back in my bag. As I looked down, I quickly noticed that the room was empty, except for jah, Barney and me.

"Cy, this is your first big test," Barney said, turning me around. "You've got to get to the Spunk in the next few minutes. Our guys are hidden along the way and they will try to stop you. They've been told to do whatever they can to stop you. It's gonna feel like they are going to kill you. Well, they might."

He stopped and winked at me.

"Use whatever you got in that bag and in that head of yours to get to the Spunk. Got it?"

With that, he gave me one of his legendary hugs. It was weird to have a hug that felt like your mother's breasts pressing against you and the power of your father's arms around you. It was still unsettling, but comforting at the same time. Then he headed out the front door.

I turned to the ruffian and must have looked terrified.

"Cy. Look at me," he said. "You gotta go. You only have a few minutes left in this realm, but you're gonna have to fight your way out. Use the tools the wizard gave ya and I think you've got the brains to make it. Take a breath, get some balls, and run."

With that, he punched me in the shoulder and headed out in front of me.

My thoughts were all over the place.

"Okay, think. Think."

I put the bag on backwards, wearing it like a chest plate. The jacket would be hardened. Sigil did have some knives in them and now they looked longer. I put my hat on and it seemed to harden like a helmet. Thankfully I'd taken a leak because I was scared to death.

"Here I go," I said, stepping up to the front door. "God if you're there, help me. Just five blocks.'

I looked out. A clod of dirt hit right near my head.

"You's aint gonna make it!" I heard someone yell.

He called me a bunch of names to complement the dirt.

"Just stay there!"

I couldn't do anything else, except... run.

Next second, I dashed out the door and cleared the stairs. A rock hit me in the chest. Thankfully it bounced right off.

"Hey, stop. Where'd ya think you were going?"

I saw my assailant running up on me. I picked up the rock and threw it back his way. It slowed him down as he yelled a list of expletives at me. The road ahead of me seemed clear with a few streetlights that weren't broken. As I kept running, I could hear more guys running after me, yelling and throwing things. Beer cans, rocks, an old diaper, and pipes. Some hit, others missed me, but my hat and jacket seemed to keep me from getting injured, but I could still feel everything that hit me.

One, two blocks, then I headed south. Then I saw them. A whole gang with baseball bats, pipes and one even had a cricket bat? They all yelled and ran straight at me.

"Weak! Scrawny! Ain't gonna make it!" was all I could hear amongst the foul names they had for me.

As they came my way, I ran up on the porches of the houses on the street. I jumped from stoop to stoop, fell through bushes and tried to avoid this gang. But they were fast. I pulled out Sigil. I tried to get a knife out, but instead an extension became a billy club. One guy hit me across the bag with a bat. It knocked the breath of me, but I was able to clip him across the face. He fell down cursing me at the top of his lungs.

One block.

Another member of the gang threw a pipe at my head. I ducked and then a bottle with a lit rag landed near me. Thankfully the bag seemed to be fireproof. I kept running.

Two blocks.

Suddenly I felt another bat across my back and I fell over. I rolled over and saw it was jah.

"You better get going, kid. These guys can taste the blood. They want ta kill ya. Run!"

I was covered in mud and water from all of the rain. In seconds I was on my feet and running. My shoes seemed to give me some traction.

At the third block I could see The Spunk – lights on and door accessible! Except for one thing. Barney was there with a bat. I could hear the gang running upon me and there was only one choice. I got out Sigil and got the blade ready. Then I ran at Barney. He was the only thing between me and the door. I didn't want to hurt him, but I had no choice.

"Stop! You aint makin' it!" the guys yelled, closing in.

I closed my eyes and ran straight at Barney. Without warning, I felt his huge hands on the arm that was holding my weapon. He took hold of my arm and like a hammer thrower in the Olympics, this monster of a man threw me into the cafe. As he did this he turned on the gang and held up his arms.

"Stop. He made it."

The boys stopped in their tracks.

The former bodybuilder turned to me.

"Fight on, Cyrus Rover. Fight on."

Then he closed the door of the cafe. I could hear the ring of the bell as it shut.

As I caught my breath, I finally stood up and realized I was in the foyer of a palatial building that looked as if it had been made into a school. But the building wasn't what captured my attention because I was surrounded by a crowd of students who all looked like mutants.

Discover the Third Space Discussion Guide that complements this chapter and join Cyrus Rover on his journey. You'll find the QR code to access them at the beginning of the book with the "Free Gift".

11

MIKA & THE BEAST

"Oh my God, oh my God."

Mika stood at the door of the hospital room. Tears streamed down her face, and her backpack in hand.

"Oh my God, Cy. What happened to you?"

Behind her, a voice broke the silence.

"This young man survived a horrendous lesson in what happens to someone when you aren't paying attention while riding a bike," Radka said, gently walking by the young film student. "Do you know him, young lady?"

As she wiped the tears from her cheeks, Mika went back into a reserved emotional state.

"My name's Mika, I'm a..."

But the facade didn't last. She truly loved Cyrus more than she realized. They shared so much in common and enjoyed each other's company ever since the first day of film school. She didn't want to rush into anything since they were poor students. But the tears just flowed.

"Sorry, um, well, I guess Cyrus and I are friends. He hadn't been in class for days and no one knew what happened to him. Then someone said they had heard he was in an accident, but didn't know where he had been taken. Is he okay?"

The seasoned nurse just smiled.

"Ah, I was wondering when this good-looking young man would have a beautiful, young lady show up. What's your name, love?"

"Um, Mika. Yeah, Mika. Beautiful? Don't think so. Besides, we are just friends," she said as she wiped away more tears and coughed uncomfortably.

The compliment caused her to look down, even though all she wanted to do at that moment was hold Cyrus' hand.

"What... what happened? What's wrong with him?"

Radka went to the corner, grabbed a tissue box, and handed a tissue to Mika.

"Hmmm, those are 'friend' tears, young lady?" she said, making quote signs with her fingers. "Why don't you come over here, out of my way, and hold his hand. The fingers on this hand weren't broken. I think having you hold his hand will help with his recovery," she said with a slight grin that hid a romantic side of her soul.

Mika gingerly sat on the chair next to the bed, and looked up to the nurse. She gently held Cy's hand. It was warm but lifeless, which made her a bit uneasy.

"Don't worry, he's aware you're there, I think," Radka said as she took Cyrus' vitals. "I can't go into all the details, but he has been in a coma since arriving," she continued. "He rode face-first into a delivery truck, but his lack of recovery has perplexed the staff. He's healthy and seems fine, but this guy has not responded to anything since being brought to this floor."

As she finished the quick check-up, she stood before the young pair with crossed arms.

"You can stay as long as visiting hours are on, which should be for the next two hours," the nurse said. "Take some time. Talk with him or just be there. It has to be good for him."

"Um, thanks," Mika called quietly as Radka headed towards the door. "Can I ask you two things, ma'am?"

"Ha, ma'am," Radka smiled. "Wow, you must have been raised right, Mika. Anything. What did you need to know?'

The nurse couldn't help but smile as she thought how respect was lost on this generation.

"Yeah, what's your name? You've been so nice. Thank you," Mika replied. "Also, Cyrus and I watch movies together. We're film students. Can I show him some of his favorite movies? I've got them on my computer."

She didn't stop holding Cy's hand, but looked the nurse straight in the eye.

"Love, as long as you keep it down, watch away. I hope it helps. My name is Radka, but my friends call me Raddy."

She smiled and nodded her head, giving Mika permission to do the same. This caused Mika to smile, even though tears still streamed down her cheeks.

"Thanks, Miss Raddy. I'll keep the volume down. Did you say I have two hours?"

She laughed and handed Mika another tissue.

"Just Raddy, and it's lovely meeting you, Mika. Yes, two hours, but if you stay a little longer, I won't say anything."

The nurse put her finger to her lips and made the 'shh' motion, and with that she closed the door and headed to the patient in the next room.

"Cy, I'm so sorry. I'm so sorry. I would've been here earlier. I... I... didn't know,' Mika said, reaching out and touching his face where the bruises remained, where he had hit the truck. "I went to your apartment to see if you were there, since it's our normal movie night. Your roommate said where you were since no one at the school seemed to know why you weren't in class."

Mika took a deep breath and looked at Cyrus in his bed. This wasn't what she had expected when she went to his place. They weren't a couple, but he usually checked in with her if they didn't have class together. So, when her friend started ghosting her, she thought it was strange, especially when he didn't show up at class. Instead of pestering him on his phone, Mika had decided to go to his apartment. If Cy acted all casual about it, she would too. Then when his roommate had said where he was, her mind raced to the worst-case scenario. Now she sat alone at his bedside, holding his hand, but not knowing if he even knew she was there. It all had that 'While You Were Sleeping' vibe, but with fewer pratfalls.

"Okay, you big jerk, you can't miss our movie night," she said as she wiped away a few more tear. "You promised me that you'd watch the X-men films with me.

Do you remember? Bryan Singer's commentary of society wrapped up in a movie franchise."

What was she doing, she wondered? Talking to someone who couldn't respond and may not even know she was there? This caused her to put his hand down on the bed as she got out her computer.

"I didn't ask, but I brought some popcorn. Now that I see you like this, well, more popcorn for me. Your loss, Cy,' she giggled.

Mika moved the table meant for food over to the bed, set the computer on top, started the film, and grabbed his hand.

Not the most comfortable chair, she thought, but this feels right.

***

I stood up and looked down at myself. My bag was a state-of-the-art backpack, I was wearing a finely tailored suit on, and as I touched my face, I felt a pair of glasses. Still, my appearance stood out because I was covered with fur.

What the hell? This had to be the strangest genre jump of them all. As I processed this whole experience, I heard a voice next to me.

"Are you okay, bud?"

Standing next to me was one of the students with a smirk on his face. It wasn't until he did a few quick laps around me to show off that I knew what he was. He was the typical speedster in most superhero storylines. Why did they always have to be so arrogant and cheeky? But it didn't matter, all I could do was play along.

"Yes, I'm fine," I said, taking it all in and not sure what to do next. "I just wasn't expecting to be here right now. Um, could you give me your name again? I must have hit my head at some point."

"Listen furball, you may be brilliant," he laughed, "but you can be such an idiot at times. How can you have all of those brains and not keep to your schedule or remember your friends? I'm only one of your best friends, remember? Hermes. You always call me Worm, you jerk."

The speedster had a look of concern in his eyes, but it faded as he winked at me.

"You're supposed to be in a meeting with the headmaster right now. His excellency sent me to find you."

He rolled his eyes and nodded down the hall.

"He's in his office. Better get moving brainiac."

With that message, the fast-talking teen was off.

"Wait, Hermes, I mean Worm! Where's…"

But it was too late. The fast-talking and running kid was gone as quickly as he had arrived. I would have to find the headmaster's office on my own. Then without any warning, someone took my hand. As I looked down, there was a stunning young woman who resembled – it couldn't be, Mika? I shook my head and looked again. Yeah, it was unmistakable. Mika, but as a mutant in school attire. What's going on? I wondered.

"Hey, you look lost, big man," she said. "Can I take you to the headmaster's office?"

I felt a spark go through my fur that seemed to come from her fingers. This shocked me awake and helped me to get my composure. My spine went straight up and a comforting feeling rushed through my body.

"That would be wonderful, thank you," I said. "Mika?"

She looked at me confused, "Ugh, yeah. Mika is still my name. Did you hit your head or something?"

As we walked down the hall, she told me about the day at this school for students with special abilities. She even shared how she had been working on her skills in controlling electrical currents. The way she held my hand, it was like we were close, even though I was inexplicably covered with fur.

I wasn't sure when we would get to the headmaster's office, so I spoke up, "Um, sorry to interrupt, it sounds like you have a busy day ahead. Can I ask you a strange question?"

We stopped and she looked at me, then shared something quite surprising. It was like she broke the fourth wall and read my mind.

"Cyrus, everyone knows why you're here. You are the center of the story and one of the smartest individuals in the building. I'm here to help and to comfort you. But you've got to keep moving to the headmaster's office. Your fur is just to help you realize where you are and what genre you have entered. Admittedly, I kinda like it. Anyway, we need to get you to your appointment. Okay?"

"Yeah, thanks. That helps. Can you hold my hand? It does comfort me."

I looked ahead and she kept talking about her day.

***

As the movie played, Mika could swear she felt Cyrus squeeze her hand. It distracted her from the film for a minute. It almost felt like a spark.

Nah, it must have been wishful thinking, she thought.

Mika sat back in the chair and got drawn into the world of mutants, heroes, and superpowers.

12

TWO VOICES

This felt good, especially since my world was all discombobulated given I had just escaped a bloodthirsty gang. To be holding Mika's hand was calming. That is, until I thought about the fact that I was a massive furry mutant. Nothing made any sense except being here with her.

"We're here," she said, letting go of my hand.

Then the beautiful mutant did something unexpected. She kissed my cheek. My furry cheek.

"The headmaster will explain everything," she said. "Take care Cy."

Yet, before she left me, I felt that spark again. It electrified my fur but didn't hurt. Then Mika was gone, and I was left looking at the ominous doors of the headmaster's office.

***

"Come in, Cyrus. Come in. You are late. We have so much to cover. Close the door behind you, please"

I was wondering which version of headmaster would be sitting there. It was no surprise that it was Elijah, but quite different than before. He was in a finely tailored suit, with an impressive haircut and his language was more refined. Yet, it was undeniable that I was looking at my genre-jumping guide. His office was grand, but had that welcoming feel you'd expect from a schoolmaster. I stepped into the office and closed the door behind me.

"Sure, sorry I'm late," I said. "I ran into problems on the way here."

I laughed uncomfortably as it hit hard all that had happened in the last few days. I guess they were days, I couldn't really tell. Then I finally got my emotions under control and I headed into the room.

The walk across the office took forever, and I could see two tall wing-backed leather chairs that faced the headmaster's desk. As I walked between them, I noticed someone else was in the room and sitting casually in one of the chairs – Barnabus! Except this time, he was fit and as well-dressed as Elijah. He sat with his legs crossed with a cup of tea on the stand next to the chair. He rested both arms on the chair and formed a triangle with his fingers. It was similar to the gesture in the dystopian chapter of this journey, but for some reason this version of Barnabus was more intimidating. As I sat in the opposite chair, my friend merely nodded at me. He wasn't as welcoming, and he looked visibly upset.

"Cyrus," he said with a bit of disdain in his voice and nodded at me.

He tapped his two index fingers together with an extraordinary level of contempt.

"You've kept us waiting. Don't you know that time is precious? You have some big moves to make and decisions to make."

This is when I noticed the spoon stirring his tea without anyone touching the cup. Also, the Newton's cradle balance balls device on Elijah's desk was moving, but only one ball was moving on one end as if tapping out a steady beat that conveyed an annoyance directed at me.

"Barnabus, that's enough," Elijah said, clearing his throat. "You know as well as I do that Cyrus has just arrived at the school. I'm sure he's still getting his head around his surroundings. Right, Cy?"

The ball stopped clicking and the spoon stopped stirring. This didn't calm my nerves. Instead, the silence was like a slap in the face. Yet, it served to shock me out of my stupor. I had still been processing the introductions of Hermes and Mika, only to be replaced by the intense versions of Barnabus and Elijah sitting in front of me. But what surprised me was how I responded with the educated manner of someone who had been formerly educated for years.

"Yes, Elijah," I answered. "This is all very overwhelming, but I think my current character is taking over my very being. So, let's discuss this next part of the journey, shall we?"

Before sitting in the chair, I put my bag on the floor and reached in to find the map. It was replaced with a tablet-like device with a beautiful leather cover. I sat back in the chair, crossed my legs, and set the map on my lap.

"Would it be possible to get some tea?" I inquired. "Barnabus reminded me I haven't had anything to drink since arriving."

From behind my chair there was a sultry and stern voice.

"Would you like four sugars as usual, Cyrus?"

Without warning, a woman was standing behind my chair.

"Hello, Cyrus. You don't know me, but I'm the headmaster's assistant, Sayge."

She stood next to my chair with a cup in one hand, the teapot in the other, and a smirk that showed her ability to anticipate every situation. Was it mutant abilities or just great training? I didn't care at the moment since I was so thirsty.

"Yes, thank you, Sayge," I said, sitting up and smiling. "You look lovely today. That would be wonderful."

"Ah, Cy, you're such a smooth talker. If you weren't so hairy, I'd..."

She gave a familiar laugh, winked at me and then poured the tea into the cup on the end table next to my chair.

"Thank you. Service as well as beauty."

I turned back to the ominous pair of mutants and guides.

"Now, let's get to business," I said. "What am I doing here? Why am I covered in fur? And the big question is, why is everyone in such a hurry to get me through this journey?"

As I finished, I set the map on the headmaster's desk, took the cup and saucer in hand, and sat back to take in the atmosphere while sipping my tea. Elijah smiled, while Barnabus didn't seem too impressed. Then the professor spoke up.

"As usual, all the right questions, Cyrus. Let's get started with the first two."

He walked around to me and settled close to my chair, just within reach of the tablet.

"After making it through the chapters of choice, justice, and fighting through perseverance, you now come to the knowledge stage," he explained. "Within this portion of your journey, you will be given certain knowledge of how to proceed and then a choice about what to do with this information."

The headmaster paused at this moment and flipped open the tablet. The map became a multi-dimensional hologram on the desk. I could see the different stages, the characters I had met, and even the school highlighted on the map. In the corner, I could see the legend had the words 'fight and perseverance' added in after my time with them in the last chapter.

"As you can see, you're at a crossroads on the map," Elijah said.

I could see that the map had two choices after this point. He continued.

"And that's the reason for the fur and this atmosphere. In most of these genres, you represent one of the most brilliant members of any team. His personality will help you to make the choice you need to make. In our experience, this mutant can tap into both sides of every situation and then discern the path that needs to be chosen. He's cerebral as well as primal in his responses. He might be green, blue or other colors, but most importantly he gives you extra wisdom."

At this point, Barnabus leaned forward.

"You see, Cy, there are two roads. The Maker will give you a choice. Both Elijah and I will provide you with the information, then you will decide how your journey will proceed. Both options are good, but one is better. Also, don't allow our presence to influence you. Instead, give us a chance to present each path, and then you can choose. How does that sound?"

I took another sip of tea.

"Fascinating and compelling," I responded. "Yet, before we go into these presentations, could I ask two more things?"

Both men nodded their heads in agreement. Barnabus leaned back in his chair and crossed his legs. Elijah merely straightened himself as he leaned against his desk and looked inquisitive.

"Food, and the last question, correct?" He smiled.

Ah, telepaths, I thought.

"Correct. I'm famished, but more importantly, why the urgency?"

At that moment, I heard the door open. Sayge walked in with a tray of sandwiches and various other snacks. She smiled that cheeky grin of hers. "Will this help with the conversation, Cyrus?" she asked.

She was so playful, it became distracting. I had never been interested in women during this journey, but all this flirting almost made me forget my feelings for Mika. I smiled as Mika came to mind.

"This place has to be the most transparent place on earth. No one can even think anything without someone knowing. Yes, thank you, Sayge," I said, setting down my cup and taking some sandwiches. "Now, that final question."

As I devoured the food, Elijah tried to look me in the eyes.

"Cy, if you don't complete the journey in three more days, you may never wake up in your world. This is the urgency. Barnabus wasn't angry, but concerned. Your life depends on how you respond to this choice."

I stopped chewing and set the sandwich down on my plate. At that moment, despite it being daylight outside, lightning stuck near the school.

***

After Mika left for the night, Radka returned to the room to check on Cyrus. As she left the room, she quickly prayed.

"Lord, watch over this young man. Help him to see he has a life worth living. Give him the awareness of how you love him. Heal him and direct Cyrus back to us. If Mika doesn't know you, save the soul of this young lady."

13

THE CROSSROADS

Despite my stomach aching from hunger, Elijah had my full attention. As I crossed my legs and set the plate on my lap, I got to thinking.

"Right," I said. "This is the stage in the journey where I need to apply what I've learned up to this choice, correct?"

Barnabus slapped his leg and leaned forward.

"Now Cyrus, you've got it. We need you to focus for your own sake. Both Mika and Sayge were even meant as distractions. We need you to see that you are up against forces who don't want you to complete this journey. Now let's get that hairy brain working as it does so well."

It was the first time he had smiled since I entered the room.

"Ah, I can feel the energy flowing through my old friend. Just calm down, Barney," Elijah said, smiling along with his friend. "He may be excited, but this is a tenuous choice to determine if you will wake up in the real world. Also, what sort of life you will lead if you do awaken. A bit daunting for anyone. Yet, a choice you must make – now."

The headmaster stopped and sat back in his chair as if waiting for a response. Without thinking, I had been eating the sandwich while the two men talked and was now onto my second. I was famished. This whole scenario didn't help, but the sandwiches did. It may have been my alter ego, but my appetite was voracious and all I wanted to do was eat. All the while, my brain seemed to be operating at lighting speed. So, I grabbed a few chips and some fruit and with my mouth full, now I needed to respond. I grabbed a napkin and after I wiped my lips.

"Interesting, I still think the mutant side of this persona inhabits my thoughts and actions more than I had expected," I shared my thoughts. "Cy would be freaking out, but I'm unnaturally calm at the moment."

I finished the sandwiches, then set the plate on the tray left by Sayge, and looked first Elijah and then Barnabus in the eye.

"There seems to be only one thing to do. Listen to your choice and make a decision. Can I ask something before you share the details?"

I looked for the teapot and poured myself a cup of tea.

"Would either of you like some tea? That's not my question, though."

"No tea for me," Barnabus said with impatience. "What do you need to know?"

I sipped the tea.

"Ugh, needs more sugar."

I leaned over and added two more cubes.

"Once you have shared the details," I said, stirring the tea, "can I ask for your advice?"

This seemed to surprise both men; they looked at one another.

"No one has ever asked that question, but you can," Elijah said. "We cannot decide for you, but, yes, you can ask for advice."

This satisfied my curiosity. I nodded my head as I sipped the tea, even though I was hoping to grab a few more sandwiches. My casual nature irritated Barnabus.

"If that is your only query, Cyrus," he blurted, "let's get started. Time is of the essence."

Elijah began.

"We will both present you with a scenario, and you must choose the path you think best for you and your future. We cannot tell you which is better or will ensure your existence. Barnabus will go first, and I will go second. Please leave your questions to the end. Are you ready to proceed?"

I sat back in my chair, tea in hand, feeling unusually calm.

"Let's go. Please share."

Barnabus stood up and began to pace.

"Cy – whichever you want to be called – your first option is immediate consciousness. You'll be brought back to full health. Life will return to normal, until you meet your future creative partner, and the pair of you will make your first film, which will be an unmitigated worldwide hit. This will lead you both to be taken to Hollywood to go on to produce some of history's biggest hit films. Money, fame, and awards will follow."

He paused to see if he had my attention. He had it. This was my dream. I wanted to ask so many questions, but I remained quiet.

"Yet, the cost for this life would be to forgo all of the relationships you have right now. Family and friends from this current life will fade into your past. This includes your connection with the church. Still, you get everything you have wanted in life up to this point. There will be no explanation to family or friends needed, since this will be a whirlwind of experiences. Your dream, Cyrus. Are you willing to sacrifice these relationships to fulfill your dreams?"

He finished, and the teacup and spoon on the table next to his chair flew gracefully to the tea cart. He poured himself a cup and then sat down.

"That's it, your first choice."

Without realizing it, I had put my cup on the table next to my chair, and I had formed the same triangle with my fingers in front of me as my arms rested on the arms of the chair. My brain was racing. Was the sacrifice worth achieving everything I thought I wanted – dreams I'd had in my heart ever since I first took footage on that old video camera? As I considered if I would wake up now, I wondered what could be the other option?

Almost on cue, Elijah placed himself in front of my chair. He had walked around to where I was sitting while Barnabus sat and stared. He leaned on his desk again and crossed his arms.

"Now, Cy, here is your second choice."

As he stared me in the eyes, it was both disconcerting and comforting at the same time. He could read my mind, but his look conveyed a quizzical, surprising expression.

"You will proceed to the door behind my desk. There is no guarantee of your safety, but beyond it is the potential for you to gain unspeakable knowledge. This will be a tough and challenging journey through to the end, if you make it there at all. If you achieve your final destination, you will discover the true purpose for living and with this information, at this moment, you will awaken."

Just like his friend, Elijah paused for effect and to ensure I was focused. Once he was sure he had my full attention, the schoolmaster managed to make his stare's intensity break through any other barriers of distraction in my mind.

"There are no guarantees for your future, except you will be allowed to maintain your current relationships, including with the church," he continued. "You could go on to fame and fortune or you might not. Yet, even though this path may seem less appealing and potentially dangerous, the rewards can potentially outweigh anything else this world has to offer."

After making this final statement, Elijah sat up straight and walked back to the other side of his desk.

"Cyrus, you have been given two choices. Unfortunately, you only have the next ten minutes to choose one. Ask your questions."

I sat there. The clock on the wall seemed to tick louder as the minutes passed. I tapped my fingers. Follow my dream but sacrifice my relationships? Take the path behind door number two, not knowing if I will survive, but maintaining my relationships? Oh how I wanted the dream, but was it worth the sacrifice? Sitting up straight, I had a resolve in my soul.

"The question for both of you is, what is the wise choice?"

Barnabus smiled, looked at Elijah, and nodded.

"That is the right question," the professor said. "We cannot decide for you, but I will say, look at the map."

This made me stand and look at the map. There was no longer a crossroad, but the line went to a door that looked like the one behind Elijah's desk.

"Cy, you still have to walk through the door. Yet, you have been given a gift," he said. "Knowledge and wisdom will guide you. This map will help your journey.

If you follow its guidance, you will find your destination. Also, you will take a portion of the gifts from this realm with you."

He smiled and turned his chair as if pointing me towards the door. With that inspiration, I closed the tablet and placed it in my bag. After picking up the bag, I went to Barnabus and shook his hand.

"Thank you, Barnabus. I will miss you. Even though you may not realize how you have been a help."

His smile masked a worrying look.

"I'm not sure you want to know this, but Elijah and I were given the same choice. Do you want to know what we chose?"

This caught my ear and I stopped packing my bag.

"Yes, I'd be very interested."

"I thought you would," Barnabus said, shaking his head. "To let you know, I chose the dream. Elijah chose the door he was given. We both survived and neither have regrets – at least I don't. Take that however you like. Whatever you choose, go well, I look forward to seeing where this journey takes you."

He shook my hand and sat back in his chair. This caused me to pause. Both options seem to provide some type of future. As I stood there, I looked at both men. What was I to do? I thought I knew initially, but now I was feeling the Cyrus portion of my mind wondering how either choice would be good. With my bag in hand and what I could imagine was a perplexed look behind the blue fur, I suddenly felt a hand holding mine.

I turned abruptly, and there was Mika. She must have come into the office while I was packing my bag. The young mutant looked up at me and signaled me to lean down.

"I've faith you will make the right choice," she said and, without any notice, kissed my lips.

I felt a shock that unexpectedly drew me to her instead of pushing me away. The surprise was that I hadn't ever kissed Mika before, but this did inspire me to keep this in mind, if I did wake up.

Unfortunately, the kiss came to an end, but we still held onto one another and gave each other one last hug. I needed to lift her off the ground to hold her in my hairy arms. Then I set her back down and kissed her hand as I turned to go. She let go of my hand as I walked towards Elijah. He held his hand for me to shake.

"So, Cy, what do you choose?" he asked.

"Honestly, I wish I had more time, but if I have to choose immediately, I'll take whatever is behind the door. Not sure why, but it comes down to what I value most. Right now, relationships mean too much to let them go. Also, ya gotta have a little faith, right?" I shrugged. "I could end up with the dream *and* relationships. In the end, it seems like the right option."

I shook his outstretched hand.

"You're right, you might get it all, but you could not," he said. "Cy, this will change your life either way. I can't guarantee anything after you walk through that door, but know The Maker will be with you throughout the journey. And as Barnabus spoiled the surprise," he said, letting go of my hand and offering me a wink, "I did walk through the door too."

With that, I went to the door, turned the knob, and never looked back.

As I walked through, there was a flash of light. I instantly found myself in a swamp. Like most marshlands, the light was limited and it took my eyes a moment to adjust. Off in the distance, I could see a glow from a fire coming from a small hut under an enormous tree. This was somewhere I looked forward to coming, yet dreaded experiencing.

Discover the Third Space Discussion Guide that complements this chapter and join Cyrus Rover on his journey. You'll find the QR code to access them at the beginning of the book with the "Free Gift".

14

TRAVELLING INTO THE SWAMP

"So, no real change, huh?"

Pastor Hudson looked slightly discouraged as he talked with the nurses at the floor's main desk. Radka had just come on for her shift.

"I'll have to look at his chart, but he was pretty calm," she replied. "No real change, except he does have a few flinches every once in a while. Go on in and after I've looked at his paperwork, I'll come in and check on you two."

She gave him as comforting a smile as she could.

'That'd be great," the pastor replied. "I'm fine. I just thought he'd 'ave improved by now. Wow, he must've hit that truck hard."

He waved at the team behind the desk as he turned to head to Cyrus' room. As he walked the cold and hygienically-scented hallways, the pastor needed to figure out what to say. Praying had been good, but there needed to be more. Then it hit him.

"I know. Yeah, I know."

He thought of something that might help.

"Hey there, Cy. No, no, don't get up."

He laughed to himself and grabbed a chair from the corner. As the middle-aged man sat down, Pastor Hudson took a deep breath and started talking.

"Cyrus, I'm not sure if you can hear me, but I'm going to share some things with you," he began. "I hope they help to get your thoughts and spirit in motion. Not sure if you remember Tyler Smith, but he was one of the kids that came along to our after-school program. You helped out a few times and the two of you connected because of your love for movies. For a 10-year-old, he seemed to know everything about Star Wars. You spoke his language and even helped him understand Jesus and the Holy Spirit using your Luke Skywalker and force analogy. The kid connected with you and eventually made a profession of faith in Jesus. You were part of that process."

He paused to see if there was any response. There wasn't, so the preacher kept talking.

"Well, Ty kept coming to the program after you went off to film school. He asked for you all the time. Then suddenly he stopped coming. I knew his family life was erratic since his parents had recently divorced. But, when I hadn't seen him for a few days, I thought I'd stop by his house after school. His mother said that he wasn't home and that he'd been hanging out for the past few days with some boys who played video games. She was worried, because Tyler had become non-communicative and would go straight to his room after he got home. She asked if I could do something."

Pastor Hudson paused and took a drink from his water bottle.

"I'll wrap it up. I haven't been able to catch up with Tyler yet. But I was hoping you'd be able to help connect with him sometime. Thought you'd like to know. Also, I want you to know that people need ya, Cy. Not sure what's happening with you, but fight on. Come back to us."

He stopped, wiped a tear from his eye, bowed his head, and prayed.

***

Without warning, there was a thunderclap, and lightning shattered the sky. This made the little hut even more visible. I started running across the marshy soil toward the building. As I ran, I noticed how things had changed. My bag was a sturdy leather backpack, my gear looked like something from a futuristic time. I could have been on any set that felt like a combination of interstellar worlds, unrecognizable creatures and plants. Still, the soil felt like the spongy marshlands close to my grandparents' house.

I finally reached the cottage. Despite the mud and damp smell, I felt good as I knocked at the door. There were noises inside, the sounds of small feet on a wooden floor. Then the door opened and there was the funniest scene I had experienced on the journey.

There was Elijah, but in miniature. He just shook his head and waved me in.

"Okay, get all the laughs out now. This is my least favorite chapter. For some reason they always make me into a smaller version of myself. Anyway, come in. Looks like you made the right choice."

He left the door open, turned, and walked towards the table in front of the fireplace.

"Close the door behind you. Some of the creatures on this planet can get in and it is impossible to get them out of the cabin. Join me at the table, we have quite a bit to cover."

Elijah pointed at a seat at the small table. He pushed a bowl of what looked like stew toward me. Something that looked like homemade bread was on a board on the table.

"Eat, my friend. You're going to need your energy during this portion of the journey."

I sat down on the low stool.

"Thanks, Elijah"

He sat down on the other stool and gently pushed the bread towards me also.

"Thanks, I just ate before showing up at your doorstep. I've got so many questions for you."

I removed my helmet and set it on the table, then set my bag on the floor. He had an irritated look on his wrinkled face.

"Cyrus, eat," he sighed loudly. "I'm telling you that you are going to need sustenance. We will have time for your questions. We will be running and talking. We will talk about the Spirit along the way. This meal will prepare you for the run.'

He pushed the bowl and bread toward me again.

"Okay, I'll eat," I relented. "But as I do that, can you explain what will happen next?"

I took a sip of the soup. It was delicious and tasted like a flavorsome beef stew. I was not sure I wanted to know what the meat was in the soup. I took some of the bread and as it hit my tongue, there was an overwhelming reminder of my grandmother's homemade sourdough. Also, something else happened as I ate. There was something like an energy flowing through my veins; the more I ate, the more energized I became. This made me eat ravenously as the Jedi spoke.

He shared with me that this stage of my learning was physical and spiritual. He would clarify the value of my physical health along with understanding the Spirit while overseeing me on this journey. In particular, how to tap into it as I headed off to subsequent phases. The only thing that bothered me was when he spoke of the next portion of this training, he seemed to hide a worried look.

As I finished the soup and bread, he poured me a liquid that looked like wine but had an effect like drinking a sports drink after a hard workout. I could feel the energy coursing through my body like nothing I'd experienced.

"Good, we're ready to roll," he said.

He brought over a backpack that looked like one of those carriers that parents put babies in. I started to laugh.

"Do we need a diaper bag for this excursion. Have you gone potty?"

I couldn't help myself and started laughing.

"Laugh it up, Cyrus. Just remember I'm going to be riding on your back and know the long way and short way to our next stop," he said, gesturing at the backpack. "Your bag will fit below the seat. No diapers, smart guy. Let's get started."

I placed the backpack on my shoulders like I knew what he was saying. As I was putting the carrier on, I could hear him shuffling through things out of my eyesight. Then the smaller version of Elijah flipped himself straight into the pack.

"Run, Cyrus. Run."

He paused.

"Yeah, the movie reference was intended. Take it however you want, but no more short jokes, or I'll keep the Forrest Gump references coming. Got it?"

Elijah had a sarcastic tone that accompanied his direction.

I made a mental note to stop making the short jokes. We headed out the door and I could finally see the trail I hadn't seen before. Without hesitating, I jumped off the house's deck, and we headed into the swamp.

15

POWER

I wasn't sure if it was the stew, drink, or a combination of both with Elijah sitting on my back, but I was energized and could finally see the path before me. The question running through my mind was where was I going? While I ran through the swamp, my mentor kept talking to me. Unlike movies that discussed the other spiritual forces as the driving power of the universe, this version of Elijah spoke of the energy found in the work of the Spirit of The Maker. He spoke with the same intensity and passion as Pastor Hudson. He never skipped a beat, even while I traversed the terrain and jumped over fallen trees

Elijah's words differed from when I sat listening to Pastor Hudson because now I was focused – laser focused. My heart was racing, but I seemed to hear every word he spoke, and each soaked into my thoughts. As he went on, he explained how the power of the universe was found in this Spirit. He was part of a trio formed into a perfect union by The Maker, His Son (who was known by a different name in our world) and this Spirit. This team was so in sync that they operated as one.

Each member of this powerful trinity had a role, and this spiritual entity was the one who guided those who believed in The Maker. Elijah said that his purpose was to help me get attuned to the Spirit's power and how to be directed by him. I thought it was interesting that he kept referring to the Spirit as a 'he.' But this wasn't my main question. I could understand how he was meant to guide me through this spiritual journey, but he had also mentioned confronting my past. What did that have to do with anything?

"Stop, Cyrus. Stop here."

Elijah pulled on the straps of the pack like they were reins. I came to a sudden stop in front of a small building. As soon as I came to a halt, my passenger jumped out and walked up to the steps. He had something under his arm.

"Come. We have arrived."

I set the carrier on the post out front and traversed the small staircase. The building looked humble on the outside since it was covered in years of swamp vegetation. All that was visible was a veranda-like flooring that led to a small wooden door. Elijah walked in, then turned and gestured for me to come through the door. Who was I to question the master? I went through the plain opening and found myself in an unearthly cathedral.

The beauty was unlike anything I had seen on screen or off screen. Unlike the murky, damp, moldy world surrounding it, the air was fresh and the light was beautifully warm, but not overwhelming. Once my eyes adjusted, I could see that we were in a room of celestial gold and ornaments that would have made the Sistine Chapel seem ordinary by comparison (I'd seen pictures). In the middle of the ornamental structure was a table, where Elijah stood. Also, what surprised me was that on the altar-like piece of furniture, I could see that he had opened a book. Was that my map? I hadn't taken it out of my bag in this world, but it had a familiarity to it that made me recognize it as I walked up to the table.

"Hey, is that my map... I mean my book?"

I looked down at it with wonder. The book was beautiful and seemed to mirror the room we had entered. It was ornate beyond recognition but for the pull it had on my soul. All I wanted to do was open it and find out what was inside.

"In this building, your map turns into a book where you can find the Truth."

My new friend spoke and it all came through clearly to me.

"Cyrus, unlike anything else in this world. It is a gift. The Spirit works through this book. You must read it. I will leave you to read and come back soon."

Now this was more of a challenge than I wanted to admit. I hated reading. I'm a visual guy, hence film. But who was I to argue with Elijah who had infiltrated my life? As I looked to respond, he was suddenly gone. The book was open and strangely drew me in.

Without realizing it, I was transfixed by the words of the map-turned-book. Nothing about this seemed odd. Unlike most other books, this one didn't cause me to get tired. I wasn't even aware I had sat in a chair near the table. Time flew by, and I devoured the words of this book that had stories, wisdom literature, and even pointed toward future events. Within it, I was able to understand more about The Maker, His Son, and the role of the Spirit.

The stew or drink might have been driving me forward through the reading. Yet, it was amazing and made things so clear. I had clarity in my mind, unlike anything I had experienced before. You could even say that the words swept over my soul like a wave and affected me deeply. I laughed, cried, and developed a resolve while reading more about the Son's work.

***

"Cyrus. Wake up."

Elijah was standing near me; I must have fallen asleep while reading.

"We have to go."

I stretched and yawned. I don't think I had ever slept that soundly, ever.

"Wait, wait, wait! I have so many questions," I said. "Elijah, I'm filled with so much knowledge, but I have multiple questions for every answer. Can you answer these for me?"

The time at the school portion of the journey had given me a voracious appetite for knowledge. He smiled for the first time since I had entered his world.

"Answers will come, but now we must go. You must confront your past."

In his hand was the carrier, and he had put the book of the Spirit under his robe. He poked me in the arm to stand up.

"We've got to go."

"Alright, alright," I said. "But I'm going to come back to you with those questions."

I picked up the carrier and put it on my back. Elijah made his expert ninja-like move and landed in the seat. It was almost cute and made me chuckle. He slammed me on the back of the head and pointed to the door. I looked back at the room's beauty to capture one last look before we headed back into the swamp.

The smell hit me first and then the darkness forced me to pause as I got used to the lack of light.

"Run, Cyrus," I heard Elijah say. "The pathway is laid out before you."

Almost instantly, I could see the path before me. Then without questioning anything, I ran. I was faster than before, but as I ran and jumped along the path my mentor kept talking. Interestingly, he answered many of my questions after reading the book. We kept going for what seemed like hours until Elijah told me to stop. He pulled back on the straps again, and I quickly halted.

There before me was a cave. As we approached the entrance, Elijah jumped out of the harness and I set it on the ground.

"Your past awaits, Cyrus," he indicated. "This is a path you must walk alone."

He held the carrier and handed me my book. At that instance, lightning lit up the sky over our heads.

***

"Please help Cyrus to recover. Lord, we have so much to do. Please let my son recover."

Cyrus' father, Rafe Rover, stood over him in the hospital with a tear rolling down his face.

16

RAFE ROVER

Rafe Rover had met Cyrus' mother, Evangeline when they attended university. She'd been studying art history while Rafe was in his final year of a film degree. His goal was to head to Hollywood as soon as he had finished his studies. The film and media department was one of the top programs in the country, and he had made his presence known with his cinematography skills. Most students wanted to be directors, but Rafe loved the nuances of setting the scene for others to build their stories upon. During his years in the department, he was part of three film projects. One had been sent by his managing professor to various film competitions.

Still, the young film student didn't have much interest in the industry politics. His main desire was to create the artistry that brings screenplays to life. During this final year, a young art student caught his attention at one of the campus exhibitions involving various disciplines. Evangeline was walking through a display of stills from Robert Richardson's career. As she was admiring a shot from The Aviator that was a stunning display of his work on one of Scorsese's underappreciated works, Rafe accidentally bumped into her. He had been so focused on the image that he hadn't noticed the young woman standing beside him. When he moved to his right to get a better angle on the shot, he stumbled into Evie and spilled her coffee.

"Hey, watch where you're going," she whispered, since the exhibition was in the university library.

Initially, Rafe was irritated and had intended to ignore her, until he turned around and saw her for the first time. He never forgot that moment. Even though he admired the artist he had come to see and was in awe of the award-winning cinematographer's work, nothing could have prepared him for the beauty of this young woman. She was stunning without having to make any effort. She had perfect proportions for a university student, but her eyes transfixed his gaze and caused him to pause his life. Everything stood still at that moment. Unlike any other occasion he could remember, Rafe was short of words and had forgotten where he was at this point in his life. He couldn't stop staring at her.

"Sorry. Really, I'm so sorry."

His response was a bit too loud, and he heard a few shushes in the hall on the other side of the artwork. Evangeline looked at him with a perplexed look as she tried to wipe the drops of coffee off of her hand. She put her finger up to her lips and made a gentle shushing sound.

"Shh, it's okay. Not a big deal," and she started to walk away.

Suddenly, Rafe came to his senses. He couldn't let her get away.

"Wait."

Again, he was a bit too loud. The shushes became louder and there was even a soft 'shut up' behind the barriers.

Evangeline turned around with a confused look on her face. Rafe walked over to her and finally lowered his voice.

"Let me make it up to you. Can I get you another coffee?"

There was a pause that seemed to last for hours, while it was most likely seconds as she pondered this offer. Rafe felt like she could look straight through him to his soul. What was it about this woman? He couldn't explain the hold she had on him. As she hesitated, it gave him more time to admire her beauty which could only be described as angelic.

In a matter of seconds, the apparent coffee victim grinned.

"Alright, but I get to pick the cafe. Right?"

Now, this was the moment that he knew he was in love. Not that he believed in that love-at-first-sight crap. But she had him. His heart belonged to her even if he never saw her past this coffee incident.

"You got it. Show me the way," he said. "By the way, my name's Rafe. Rafe Rover."

He laughed with an awkwardness that was unlike him. Again, more shushes from the library, and one guy said, "Really man, be quiet, already."

"Well, Rafe, Rafe Rover," she smiled and whispered, "let's go to The Hills. Get a coffee, and I'll consider giving you my name."

"Deal."

He stuck his hands in his pockets, she threw her coffee cup in the trash bin, and they headed out of the library.

They went to an Italian-inspired cafe that was named after the hills of the Italian countryside and grabbed two cappuccinos. They continued the conversation about the Robert Richardson exhibition as they sat down, but things quickly went deeper. The coffee led to dinner, and they talked into the evening. During the dinner, Andre Bocelli's version of *Vivo per Lei* played in the background and set the tone for the night. Both admitted that moments like this were not typical for either of them. Still, it was a magical night until they realized the time, and they both had early classes.

Rafe paid, and they headed back towards campus. As they walked back, they kept talking about their lives, and finally, without any prompting, she spoke up.

"Evangeline. My name is Evangeline Fremont. Most people call me Evie."

"Well, Evangeline 'Evie' Fremont," Rafe replied, making the quote symbol with his fingers as he said her nickname, "it's wonderful to meet you. Can I ask for another 'coffee' soon?"

He did the quotes symbol again and regretted it later. She made him nervous and vulnerable all at the same time. She giggled as she came to a stop.

"Here is my building. Yes, Rafe. Rafe Rover. I'd like that. Friday?"

He tried not to jump in the air with all of the emotions he seemed to be experiencing like it was the first time.

"Friday. Meet you here? 5pm?"

"Friday, 5pm. Right here," she said, pointing to the spot on the sidewalk. "Hold out your hand."

She took a pen out of her bag, wrote her phone number on his hand, gently folded it closed, and then kissed him on the cheek. Then without a word, she turned and went into the hall.

Rafe must have stood there for quite some time. He was stunned, his heart racing.

What just happened? he thought. I just met the girl of my dreams.

He finally started walking and headed toward his apartment complex. Nothing else seemed to matter as he strolled along the path that worked its way through the campus.

***

Friday couldn't arrive soon enough. Rafe met up with Evangeline, and this was the beginning of their whirlwind romance. Over the weeks after their fateful coffee meeting, between art and film projects, they did all they could to find time for one another. They talked about their dreams, future, and how they could fit into one another's plans. The semester flew by, and they moved from young love to being lovers. It was unexpected for both of them, mainly since Evie had grown up in a conservative Christian home. Yet, they could only think about their love for one another and how nothing would get in the way of this bond.

That was until, one day, when Rafe's professor announced (in their final class) that the project he and his classmates had sent in, (for the film competition) had won the grand prize. The student filmmakers would be flown to Los Angeles to receive the award, meet the executives behind this competition, and then see what opportunities would arise.

Rafe was thrilled, and the only person he wanted to tell was Evie. After class, he ran to her building and called her from the phone in the lobby.

"I've got something to tell you, can you come down?"

She paused.

"Yes, I've something to tell you too," she finally said. "Be right down."

They walked to the cafe, where they first got to know one another. After getting their drinks, they sat down at their table. Rafe started.

"You okay? You seem kinda quiet. What did you want to tell me?"

Evie took a sip of her coffee.

"No, no. I'm fine. Tell me what you want to tell me first. You look so excited."

He went on to tell her what his professor had told him about the trip. The team who made the film would fly out in a couple of days for Los Angeles and would even be permitted to forgo the final exam. It was a prestigious prize for the film department, and the leadership wanted the students to take advantage of every opportunity.

"Ah, so you fly out soon. Will you be coming back?"

Evie took another sip of her coffee but seemed to be holding back tears. Rafe reached out and held her other hand.

"Evie, of course I'll be back. These things usually don't lead to much. I wish I could take you with me. No need to cry, I'll be back. I'll return for you."

He held her hand and looked into her eyes.

"Now, what did you want to tell me?" Rafe said, looking at her expectantly.

"Oh, nothing important," she said, grabbing one of the napkins from the holder on the table. "I need to go home this weekend. That's all."

"All okay?" Rafe said, confused. "Everything okay at home?"

"Yeah, yeah. Everything's fine," Evie assured him. "I just need to take care of things with my parents. I'm fine. Really. Let's go get something to eat to celebrate. Okay?"

She stood up.

"Are you sure you're okay, Evie?" Rafe said, his look going from confusion to concern.

"Absolutely. Let's celebrate. You deserve it."

Evie squeezed his hand and encouraged him to stand up. They hugged and went out the door. They celebrated into the night, Rafe flew out later that week, and Evie went home over the weekend.

***

Rafe never returned. The film was a triumph in filmmaking, and the executive team offered him an apprenticeship with one of the studios. It was just the beginning of things that would lead to Rafe becoming one of the leading cinematographers of his generation. Initially, he called Evie every day and promised to return to get her. Yet, as he buried himself in his work, the calls became less frequent, promises were broken and they quickly lost touch.

As the years passed by, if there were any regrets for Rafe, they would be how he had left things with Evie. Rafe became so immersed in his work that he hadn't done much to follow through with their relationship. He eventually went on with his life and lost touch with the beautiful young woman he met at the Robert Richardson exhibition.

***

Evie had lied; she meant to tell Rafe that she was pregnant. She wanted to tell Rafe but seemed to know she had lost him to his dream. Even during some of the calls where he promised to come and get her, she knew that their relationship was over. Her decision to not tell Rafe about their child was emotional and rash. Still, Evie thought she was protecting her baby and herself from heartbreak.

After Rafe had flown out and as the semester came to an end, she packed her things and headed home to her parents. Her life would be changed forever, but Evie was determined to keep the baby. Her parents loved her through the pregnancy and never asked her to leave their home. They helped her to raise Cyrus after he was born.

From the moment Cyrus was born, the young mother knew she had made the right decision. Her love for her son knew no limits; she even forgave Rafe for leaving her to fend for herself. This led to her deciding to include Rafe's name on the birth certificate. Hence the reason why Cyrus carried his name. Still, she never contacted the young man she met at the Robert Richardson exhibition.

Evie always planned to tell Cyrus about his father, but she tragically died in a car collision one night when she was coming home from work at the local art gallery. Her son was only a toddler then, and the accident left her parents to care for Cyrus as they grieved the loss of their only daughter. They thought it would be best if their grandson didn't meet his father. This could have been due to the hurt they harbored over the death of their daughter or the overwhelming feeling of raising a boy at their age. Still, Les gave Cyrus that old camera, thinking it would connect him to his father. Even though Katy didn't want their grandson to have the camera, she went along with it, but committed to not contacting Rafe about his son.

Whenever Cyrus asked about his father, they said he hadn't been part of his mother's life. They never mentioned anything about who his father was or what he did. Even when his film studies had led him to say, "Wouldn't it be cool if Rafe Rover was my dad," the couple had dismissed the idea, laughing outwardly at the suggestion, and never said anything.

That was until one night after Cy's accident. While they were praying, the couple was prompted to contact the man who they had never met. Especially since there was nothing they could do for their grandson and there was no guarantee he was going to wake up from his coma.

It took some time, but they finally got through to Rafe, who was on location in Australia filming an outback epic. They did their best to share the details of Evie and Cyrus over the years. Transparency was the only way Katy thought she could share the story with this celebrated filmmaker. They covered everything, from University, Cyrus' birth, their daughter's death, life raising their grandson, film school, all the way up to his current condition. The whole experience was exhausting, but unusually therapeutic since they both felt like a burden had been lifted from their shoulders for the first time in years.

To their surprise, after hearing their story, they could tell Rafe was crying and quite emotional. Despite being a stranger to them and not knowing if they were legitimate, he told Cyrus' grandparents that he would be at the hospital in two days. Rafe didn't sound angry, and his words were very kind and grateful. Before he hung up the phone, Rafe offered them a heartfelt apology.

"Mr. and Mrs. Fremont. I'm so sorry. Evie was special to me, and I regret that we would have to meet this way. I hope you can forgive me, and I cannot express how much I appreciate you calling me. It will take some time for me to get to Cyrus, but I'll be there as soon as possible. I hope to meet you, too. Thank you."

They talked for a bit longer and they shared where Cyrus was hospitalized. Then he hung up and the pair hugged, cried, and went back to praying.

***

After the lightning strike, I entered the cave entrance. As I walked through the darkness, I could see someone in the back. An eerie light shone down on a throne-like chair, and a person sat upon the seat. It looked like a man with an elegant robe with a hood covering his face. Since Elijah hadn't told me what to do, I walked over to the throne.

"Hello, sir," I said. "This will sound odd, but Elijah sent me in here, and I think I'm meant to meet you."

The figure moved as if waking up from a deep sleep. He stood and approached me.

"Yes, Cyrus, I've been waiting for you."

As he walked towards me, I braced himself for whatever was about to happen. Throughout this journey, I hadn't known what to expect. I could feel the Sigil on my belt. I was going to be ready to fight if need be. Then as the man stood before me, he removed his hood, and I could see him clearly for the first time.

I looked into the face of a man who looked like an older version image of me. Taller, regal, but there was no mistaking that we shared a similar look.

"Dad?"

17

FACE OFF

Now this is new, was all I could think. Am I meant to face myself?

All I had was my weapon and my pack. My thoughts were racing. My alter-ego didn't look threatening. What was I meant to do here? This couldn't be my dad, could it? Then the man spoke.

"Cyrus, I'm your father."

"What? You're going to quote that line as an introduction?"

I was confused. My unsettling older self started to laugh.

"You're right. I've always wanted to say that line. It was the right time, wrong context. Sorry. But, really, I'm your father."

He put out his hand as if to shake my hand. As I went to shake it, suddenly chains came out from the chair he had been sitting on and wrapped themselves around the body of my father. They pulled back into the chair, and a light field appeared around him. It all happened in seconds, and the chains' force caused me to fall back onto the floor. As I picked myself up, all I could see was this man who claimed to be my father in chains, sitting in the chair, and a force field surrounded him with an eerie light. To say I was confused was an understatement. There I was, unexpectedly desperate as I walked up to the cage of light. I reached out to see if I could reach through the light.

'Ouch!'

I pulled my hand back. The field was electrified.

"Can you hear me?" I yelled, looking at the bound man in the chair.

The chains not only kept the man who claimed to be my father immobile, but the light field kept me from being able to communicate anything.

What just happened? I thought. I went from having a father to now seeing him in chains.

"Yeah, this part sucks. It is a brutal test."

Elijah made me jump out of my skin.

"What the... Oh my word. Elijah. Where'd you come from?"

"Sorry, Cyrus, but this is an important test," he continued. "You have two more genre jumps. During these times you must find the key to free your father."

For the first time I went ballistic, travelling from confused to angry.

"What? I meet my father and you chain him? What key? Genre jumps? What's going on?'"

"Did you forget so soon?" the little man said sternly. "This whole journey must include a rescue. Your map has answers and you must find the key to rescue yourself and your father."

He pointed toward the tunnel that was next to the throne that was currently imprisoning my father.

"You've got to go."

"Okay, okay. Let me think."

I set my pack on the ground and pulled out the map. It had changed back from a book to a scroll. I unrolled the scroll on the cave floor and saw a key above the map. It was at the end of the line that contained two large dots. After seeing the key, the map did something new. It shone a light towards the tunnel entrance. Also, there was something else that was added to the legend. There was a clock – one that was counting back from 48 hours. This made me look over at Elijah.

"Help me out. I'm on the clock now?"

"You've got to go. Two genre jumps, 48 hours. Your father's life depends on you. The map will guide you. It will provide the answers you need. Go now, Cyrus."

Elijah rolled up the map, put it in my pack, and handed the bag to me. That is when he pointed with his other hand toward the mouth of the tunnel. I picked up my bag and took a deep breath.

"Here we go."

I looked at the man who was meant to be my father.

"Hopefully I'll be back soon."

I put my pack on my back and turned towards the mouth of the tunnel, gathered my wits and ran. As I broke through the darkness, I stopped short and saw a cavern before me with another tunnel on the other side. Who was standing on the other side?

He looked like Elijah dressed as an adventurer, and he seemed to be waving me forward.

Thank God I had stopped in time! The cavern below me didn't seem to have a bottom. Yet, now what was I supposed to do? On the other side of the gap was a man who looked like a weathered and experienced version of Elijah. He cupped his hands around his mouth like he was instructing me. At least he was full-sized in this portion of the journey.

As I looked down, I noticed I was wearing 1940's explorer's gear. I felt my head and discovered I was wearing a fedora. My bag had transformed into a weathered leather satchel. I decided to cup my hands around my mouth and I yelled.

"What're you saying??"

Then I put my hand up to my ear.

"You've got to believe, boy," I heard Elijah yelling. "It's a leap of faith!"

It was definitely his voice.

I was trying to remember what film this scene was from and vaguely remembered the moment. The protagonist had needed to step out in faith to save his father. At that moment, I could see Elijah on the other side beckoning me to come. But this was crazy, I thought. All I could see was my imminent death before me.

"C'mon! You've gotta step out in faith! Time is running out, Cyrus!" My khaki-clad friend called.

He was noticeably frustrated and urging me to join him. I guess he was my friend, sometimes it was hard to tell.

There was sweat running down my face, but all I could do was think about the man who was said to be my father – chained, and me with only 48 hours to save his life. Shaking, terrified and going against every thought of safety, I finally decided to step out into the void. Gravity pulled me down...

Thankfully, it was only inches before I felt solid ground under my feet. Despite not seeing it, there was a narrow stone path beneath me. It had a mirrored effect on top, making it virtually impossible to know until you were on it. Not that it made it any less terrifying. Still, I kept my eyes on the man in the crevice on the other side. I walked carefully at first but eventually got up speed and reached out for Elijah. He grabbed my hand and pulled me through the opening to the new tunnel.

"There you go, boyo. Well done. Scary as hell, but worth the ride. Typical day in the life of exploration and adventure. This is a fun segment, but time is moving fast. Let's get inside and then I'll explain why you're here."

He led the way into a corridor that opened onto a large room with multiple doors. After getting my head straight and realizing what was happening, I finally spoke up.

"I'm sorry, but my head is all over the place. Between my dad and my heart racing after that jump, I just want to know what's going on?"

"Oh, I wish we had more time to get to know one another, but you are on the clock. All I can do at this point is explain what you need to do to get from this portion of the journey to the final destination that will give you the answers to save your father."

He reached into his pocket and pulled out an antiqued key.

"'I'm here to help," the swashbuckling version of Elijah said, handing me the key, "but I can't make the choice you need to make at this point. This key opens the door to the final stage of this quest. It's not the key to freeing your father, but it will lead to that stage. The answers to your father's release will be found there."

He paused, like a trained teacher to ensure I was listening. Once he realized I was totally committed and focused, he continued.

"As you can see there are multiple doors, but the key only opens one. I can give you three clues, but they must come in the answers to questions you ask me. After asking the questions and I answer them, you will have three opportunities to choose. Just like any set of three questions, you cannot ask the obvious question of which door to choose. You've got to figure this out on your own."

He looked at me to see if I was paying attention. I looked at the key in his hand.

"I think I've got it. But can I ask a clarifying question before asking about the clues for the door?" he said.

He sighed.

"Yes, Cyrus, as usual, you get one," Elijah replied. "You get one question of clarity – that's it. Any other questions will be taken from the three clues. Got it?"

He smiled and sat on a large rock to the side of the doors.

"I ask questions, I choose the door, I have three tries, I think that's pretty clear," I breathed deeply. "But what happens if I don't choose right?"

"Ah, consequences. Good choice," Elijah nodded. "Well, think clearly. Remember your movie history and all that Pastor Hudson taught you over the years. This will help. Also, I hope you choose well. Otherwise, your journey ends without any conclusion and your father remains imprisoned. Sorry, I wish it was less stressful, but those are the facts. Remember, you're on the clock. Better get crackin' on the questions."

Elijah expectantly leaned forward, waiting for the questions. I was pouring with sweat, but I thought about things for a minute. I reached into my satchel and pulled out the map. It was now a leather-bound diary and I opened it where there was a pen. On the page were the numbers 1, 2, and 3.

Above the letters read, 'The key to the father is found within these pages.'

18

THE DOOR

"Lord, we want to pray for our Cyrus. Please heal his body and help him to come back to us. Amen."

Katy and Les were praying for their grandson during the daily visit. Katy held Cyrus' hand, Les sat in the corner and sighed deeply since there didn't seem to be any response.

"Oh, I'm sorry, I didn't realize you were in here," Nurse Radka said, entering the room. "I can come back..."

"No, no, Radka. It's wonderful to see you," Katy replied. "We're done prayin'. Cyrus doesn't seem to have changed much. Thanks for taking care of our boy."

Katy looked at her boy and held his hand with both of her hands. The nurse stood there for a minute to take in this scene.

"It's my pleasure," she said. "I'm praying for him every day, too. I've faith he'll recover soon."

She paused, then she added, "It's strange, everything about him is fine, but something seems to keep him trapped in this coma. We'll keep praying that Cyrus will find his way home."

She went on to do her usual rounds. Katy just continued holding Cyrus' hand. Les came over and touched his wife's shoulder, and they started praying again.

"Lord, show him the way home. Show him Your way."

***

I could feel a rumbling in the cave as I looked at the diary in my hand. It was like a wake-up call to get on with the questions. Elijah sat there like a living statue waiting for the first query. He shifted his weight but didn't say anything. All I could think was that Elijah must enjoy this chapter much more since he had all of the charisma associated with these men. It poured out of him as he sat there in his adventurer garb waiting to answer my questions. What would this character know about these doors, I thought. And how would he be connected with my conversations with Pastor Hudson. What was the connection?'

"Adventure. History. Doors. That's the connection," I blurted out suddenly.

Elijah adjusted himself and looked towards me.

"Was there a question in that outburst, Cy?"

"No, no… not yet. But, I think I've got it."

I started to scribble something in my diary. Then the pen began to write for me. I looked up in amazement.

"Elijah, my first question is to help me to know where I'm going – so how can I know the way?"

The explorer slid his hat back on his head and let loose a big grin.

"That's it, kiddo, you've got this. The door you seek is the way and the truth and the life. No one can find the path without going through this door. What's your next question?"

This answer was familiar, but after Elijah answered me, something else happened. Some of the doors disappeared and the remaining ones reshuffled on the wall. All I could do was think harder.

Ah, all I need to do is remember what Pastor had taught me, I thought. Doors… Entry…

"Lord help me. Show me the way to the key and home."

The words surprised me as they came out of my mouth, since I hadn't thought to pray at all during this journey.

"Sorry, mate. What'd you say?" the adventurer asked, sitting forward a bit and adjusting his whip on his belt.

I looked down at the book and saw the pen was writing frantically.

"Right," I smiled. "How can I have life, and have it to the full?"

"The doorkeeper opens the door for you, and those who hear his voice and listen will know the voice and know which way to go," Elijah replied. "The doorkeeper is the door too; if you open this door and walk through it, you will be free. Well done, Cy. You've got one more question."

The man stood with an uncharacteristic anticipation. It was motivating to see him excited. Especially as more doors disappeared and only three remained.

As he got excited, I almost wanted to choose from the remaining three doors. I even closed the diary and looked at the remaining entry points. One was opulent and grand, the next was beautifully crafted as if made by a master carpenter. It had been built with an attention to detail unlike any I had seen before. This door caused me to step forward until I noticed Elijah's expression change from excitement to frustration. Suddenly the ground rumbled under my feet. Both things caused me to pause and shake my head as if coming out of a trance. I still had one question.

The third door wasn't anything special, and all it managed to do was cause more confusion than providing answers. So, I stepped back and opened the diary again. The pen leapt to life and wrote out the final question. I shook my head.

"Okay ... should I choose the beautiful door or the unassuming one that looks like a tight fit?"

Elijah came over and shook my hand.

"Enter through the narrow door," he said. "The beautiful, large doors lead to destruction, and many enter through them. But small is the door, and narrow is the pathway that leads to life, and only a few find it. Cy, you've found it. Well done. Now it's up to you to open it and walk through."

At that moment, the opulent and well-crafted doors disappeared, and the humble, narrow door was front and center.

"Thanks, Elijah," I said, shaking the guide's hand.

The adventurer version of my friend let go of my hand and removed his hat. "You chose well," he replied. "Stay on the straight and narrow, kiddo."

He handed me the pack he arrived with and pointed me toward the door with his hat.

"One last thing, your time is running out, but be aware of something. As you look for the key, know that the doorkeeper and the door can be the same. Can it be the key also?"

"What do you mean?" I said perplexed, but something in all of this sounded like he had heard it before.

"Sorry, you're out of questions," Elijah smiled, "but when looking for the key, it may not be where or even what you think it is."

I smiled an uneasy smile, put the bag on his back, and reached for the doorknob. Then I heard something that I didn't expect. Someone was knocking from the other side. I looked back at Elijah with a perplexed look. He was just smiling and shrugged his shoulders. Then a voice came through the door.

"Cyrus, come on through. We've been waiting for you."

The voice sounded inviting and comforting. After all of this adventure, nothing surprised me. Still, this made the whole thing even more unnerving.

As I turned the knob, the door opened, and I could see a path weaving through a pasture of green. There wasn't anyone there, but the atmosphere beyond the door seemed to draw me in. I looked back at Elijah and waved.

"Cyrus Rover, I always seemed to know you'd be walking through that door," he said.

He winked, and I found himself sucked into this new world.

As I looked down at myself, I noticed that my adventurer clothes had changed into an outfit from a fantasy era. I had a sword at my side, a leather bag on my back, and my jacket was a majestic-looking hooded creation of the finest fabric.

As I momentarily got my bearings, I noticed that I was near a road. Then, as I looked around, there they were, as clear as Elijah had been a minute previously: centaurs, dwarves, walking bears, and four humans who looked like royalty riding on magnificent horses. Suddenly, one of the horses spoke up.

"Make way, sir, these are the kings and queens of this land. Make way, sir."

Discover the Third Space Discussion Guide that complements this chapter and join Cyrus Rover on his journey. You'll find the QR code to access them at the beginning of the book with the "Free Gift".

19

IN THE PRESENCE OF THE KING

id that horse just talk?

I got out of the way of the entourage that surrounded this land's supposed royals. It all looked familiar to me because of some of the films I had watched growing up. Also, Pastor Hudson's kids always talked about a book series like this one.

The horse continued to look at me as I tried to stay outside the path of the rest of the princes' and princesses' followers.

"Boy, what are you doing on the ground? Are you friend or foe?"

I was confused and scared.

"I guess a friend," I said, managing to get the words out.

The horse remained focused on me as the rest of the company continued to travel up the road.

"Um, I'm new to this land and I'm not sure I know whose side I'm on, but I know I'm not a foe."

I slowly put my pack on my back as I faced off against the intense gaze of this massive stallion.

"Oh yeah, Cyrus Rover. That's my name."

This seemed to settle the magnificent animal. Then, for the first time, I saw the man riding him.

"Master Cyrus, it is good to make your acquaintance" he said, winking at me.

To my surprise, Barnabus was riding the talking horse and he seemed thrilled to see me. His look was similar to that during my time on the porch, eventually at Spunk Café, and finally at the school for mutants.

"They call me Prince Barnabus in this land," he said jovially, "and you have now met the legendary war horse, Ardan."

Barnabus looked great in his royal clothing and carried himself with unwavering confidence but seemed to have a disarming softness as well.

"Great to see you Barn... I mean Prince Barnabus. And it's an honor to meet you Ardan," I said

I added a bow in for good measure. The horse seemed to let out a laugh with a whinny attached.

"Boy, you need not bow to us. Prince Barnabus is royalty, but we both appreciate those who are new to our magical land. Stand up. Are you going to the festivities?"

"Master Cyrus, forgive my friend," Barnabus added. "He has the manners of a plow horse some days."

"I beg your pardon, at least I don't let the castle winery distract me," Ardan said, shaking his mane and snorting.

They both laughed.

"Sorry, my good man, there is a bit of history between us, though the jokes may not be that funny to you," Prince Barnabus explained. "My apologies, what my friend meant to ask is if you would like a ride to Asaph for the games?"

He looked down at me. I was still taken aback by what was happening before me. A man and a horse conversing and joking like old friends? I finally shook myself awake.

"Yes, Prince Barnabus, I'd appreciate a ride. Also, could you help me know more about where I am?"

"Ah, I think Fireinder might be the right one for this task," Barnabus said, signaling for another horse to come up.

Within moments, a gorgeous mare came galloping up to the prince and his horse. I could only wonder why there was a horse without a rider available?

This magnificent creature allowed me to ride on her back to Asaph and ride along wherever they went. Fireinder was also patient with me since I had no experience riding. She was a talking horse, too. We traveled along the road with the small band of warriors that seemed to be waiting for Prince Barnabus.

As we worked our way towards Asaph, Fireinder endured my unexpected handling. We quickly learned a bit about one another and the details of this strange land that included talking horses, centaurs, and other bizarre beasts making their way to Asaph. I felt nothing could be more irregular than how I came here. So, I decided to share most of my journey with the majestic horse.

"Ah, your story is like the kings and queens who entered this world through the legendary passageway," she reflected. "We must introduce you to them once we arrive at the castle."

Fireinder went on to tell me about the land I had fallen into and gave me a condensed version of the tales of the past. She shared about fauns, witches, and other magnificent creatures. I even heard some creatures say, "Thank The Maker." It reminded me of how my grandparents would say "Amen" when someone mentioned God in a story. It was strange.

I finally settled into the saddle and enjoyed the conversation. I hadn't had an extended conversation with someone or something for a long time. Fireinder seemed to enjoy the discussion, too. It was pretty refreshing, and the time went by quickly. We arrived at the gates of the majestic city quickly.

As we entered the city's walls, the soldiers stood at attention as Prince Barnabus rode by on Ardan. Barnabus signaled me to come up next to him, and Fireinder and I trotted toward my new royal friend.

"Thanks Fireinder, you've served our new friend quite well. Especially since this was meant to be a break for you during this journey. We thank you."

Barnabus nodded his head towards the horse, as if in reverence.

"It was actually a joy," the beautiful creature said, seeming to bow her head. "Also, this young man seems to have quite a story to share. He comes from a magical land similar to our current monarchs. Yet, his accent is very different, and his journey has involved many stages that I'm not sure I understand. He kept talking of moving pictures and mentors."

"We will have to see if we can have him share his story with us all," the prince replied.

I was mesmerized by the castle and the crowd of mythical creatures that walked through the streets as though everything was normal. I hadn't heard the interchange between the young prince and his horse. There were talking bears and figures I could only assume were naiads and dryads. An imposing creature that had to be a minotaur walked by me and I shivered with fear as he stared at me.

"Master Cyrus, Master Cyrus," Barnabus said, trying to get my attention. "Cyrus, can you hear me, young sir?"

As the latest immigrant to this strange land, I shook myself out of my staring fest with the terrifying beast.

"Sorry, sorry, yes. Prince Barnabus, what can I do for you? Sorry."

"Good. We've come to the castle entrance," he said, masterfully dismounting Ardan. "Let's prepare you for entering the kings' and queens' court. You can see them over in the distance as they come through the Southern gate."

I could see the banners and the regal stature of the royals as they rode into the city.

"Fireinder will remain available for you, but you must leave behind your new steed for now," he smiled. "She has taken a liking to you."

I had never ridden a horse before, so getting off the back of Fireinder was going to be a challenge. She was such a tall and statuesque animal. Suddenly, I felt her begin to kneel under me. I could step off her without much issue as she got close to the ground with her front quarters. This made me smile and I could only do one thing: my arms went around her muscular neck to show my gratitude.

"Thank you, my new friend," I said, patting her on the side. "Fireinder I can only imagine that you deserve more respect than I can give you. Still, I hope we will come together again."

The noble animal whinnied and then looked her rider in the eye.

"I cannot explain the connection, but you have my loyalty, Master Cyrus," she replied. "If things go well with the kings and queens, we may serve together again."

With that exchange completed, I looked over to Barnabus and the royal motioned for me to come with him into the castle entrance.

"Cyrus, you must go and get changed," he said as we walked together. "There will be courtiers who will ensure you are in proper attire to come in the presence of the royals of this land."

The prince signaled for two servants to come and care for his guest.

"Thanks Barney– sorry, Prince Barnabus." I said as I was led off. "Will I see you there?"

I could see my new friend was being shepherded off himself.

"I hope to see you very soon, Master Cyrus.'"

The prince was taken off to a different room and I was escorted to my own dressing room. Honestly, I had never been treated with so much care in my life. The bustling around me was mind-boggling, but I had to trust that the servants were there to help. They washed and gave me new clothes – they even cleaned my sword. I felt fresh and uncomfortably formal when it all came to a close. Once things were completed, I was ushered out another door.

Soldiers led me down the hallway and into what could only be considered the Grand Hall. As we entered, I could see Prince Barnabus entering simultaneously with his own party of soldiers and maidens. Both groups stopped as we joined a grand circle of majestic-looking creatures who were all looking forward. Then suddenly, it was like the whole crowd reacted on cue, and there was a wave of excited gasps, and then they all bowed. I quickly looked forward too, and out of respect followed the crowd's lead and found myself bowing. Before I completed my bow, I saw what everyone was looking at on the staging at the front of the room. Within the red-brown stones and below the opulently bejeweled archway were four thrones. The four humans I had seen earlier in the day took their seats in their thrones, two men and two women of dignified stature. Even though they were impressive, they weren't the room's primary focus.

In between the four thrones sat a large throne that garnered the crowd's attention. In that opulent chair sat a meticulously dressed man who oozed confidence. Yet, he also managed to personify humility. It shouldn't have surprised me, but it did. Here sat the king above all of the rest, King Elijah.

20

THE STORY UNFOLDS

Rafe walked into Cyrus' room and stopped just inside the door. Grandma Katy was praying over his son and her grandson. The two of them had never met in person, but her call had brought him back into Cyrus' life. He had to determine if this was the right time to formally introduce himself. The filmmaker was frozen in the doorway as he listened to this woman as she prayed with a captivating passion.

"Lord, be with our boy. I come to you with these requests. My faith is in you, Jesus. Please bring our Cy back to us. Whatever is holding him back, free him. Help him to fight for life and to come back to us. Please hear my prayers. Amen."

She finished and wiped a tear from her eye with a tissue from the bed stand. Then she jumped as she finally noticed Rafe standing in the doorway.

"Oh, you startled me. Can I help you?"

She smiled with kindness and weariness that was disarming.

Now, there was no turning back, Rafe thought. He had to go to her.

"Hello, Mrs. Fremont, may I come in?" he asked. "I do apologize that I interrupted your time with Cyrus. I'm... um... Rafe Rover. You, uh, you called me."

As he stepped forward into the room, Cyrus' grandmother stood up. Unexpectedly, she met him at the foot of the hospital bed. Rafe expected a slap or some sort of verbal correction, but instead, she embraced him.

"You came, you really came. Praise Jesus. You came."

Her hug was unlike anything the man could remember. The smell of her perfume, her gentle but firm touch, and the softness of her voice calmed his soul down to his very core. It was the familiar feeling he had when he had first met Evie.

"Oh, Mr. Rover, you came. Thank you."

Katy finally let go of him and looked into his eyes.

"Mr. Rover. Please accept my apologies for not calling you sooner. Your son idolized you without even realizing you were his father. He's a film student, but I regretted that he needed his father. My anger and grief kept me from calling you sooner. Please forgive me that you have to meet your son this way. Thank you for coming, thank you."

She stared into his eyes and held his arms in the hospital room.

"Oh, no...no...I'm the one who needs to apologize," Rafe managed. "If I hadn't left Evie suddenly after university and been so self-absorbed... I wasn't even aware that Cyrus had come into the world. Please forgive me. Thank you for calling me."

He motioned for them to both sit down. At that moment Grandpa Les walked back into the room with coffee from the cafeteria.

"Oh, I'm sorry," he said, looking at the man sitting with his wife with a perplexed look.

"Les, Les, this is Rafe Rover," Katy said excitedly. "He came, can you believe it? Cyrus' father has come."

Katy was so excited she was crying, but they were obviously happy tears.

There was an awkward tension in the air. Les set the coffee cups on a stand in the corner. He walked over to Rafe with a serious look that seemed to be a strange combination of anger and joy. The senior man signaled for Rafe to stand. The filmmaker had looked into the lens at some of the greatest actors as they portrayed some of the most intense characters in movies. Yet, he had never been in a situation that shook him to his core. As he rose to face Les Fremont, Rafe found himself shaking. As he stood, Les grabbed the man's arm and then pulled him to himself. His hug was firm and undeniably intentional.

"Young man, your son needs you." he said through tears and emotion. "I've tried. Oh, I've tried to be his father for years, but this is an answer to something that I've prayed over for years. Your son needs his father. Thank you. I don't know what you've sacrificed to be here, but you've blessed us. Praise God for you."

Katy was crying even harder since she had never seen her husband hug another man or speak so many words at one moment. Rafe was overwhelmed with all of the emotion and gratuitous words, especially since he didn't expect anything from these people. Yet, their love was undeniable.

"Thank you, sir. Thank you for your kind words. Also, for caring for my son all of these years. Please, sit. Let's talk."

They all three sat down at the foot of Cyrus' bed and Rafe was able to ask the question he had sitting in the back of his mind.

"What do you mean that Cy knew who I was?"

They sat in the corner of the room and talked for quite some time. Katy explained everything that had happened to Evie and Cyrus' life. Some of it was what she had shared over the phone, but now she could add to the details. Katy explained how Les had given their grandson a camera early in his life, how Cy had grown to love film and had even pondered his connection to Rafe. Rover was a unique surname.

The filmmaker explained how his youthful pride and ambition had made him lose sight of Evie's needs. Rafe had thought there was always something he was missing in the tone of her voice, but never pursued those inclinations. He explained that while working on one production a few years ago he had struggled with his mental health. A counselor had recommended that he consider his spiritual well-being, which was when he began exploring Christianity. Initially, the filmmaker rejected most of its teachings. Still, eventually he came to see the value it had to him and had become a Christian a few years back. He was still traveling through his faith but was thankful for all it had given him.

"Mr and Mrs Fremont," He finally thought he would interject about his responsibility. "I've enquired about the costs of Cyrus' care and I'll cover any medical bills," Rafe began. "Unfortunately, the doctors and staff seem to think they have done all they can do for Cyrus. It's a waiting game. I'll admit I'm not a patient man. God is working on me. Still, if there is something else, you want me to do – different doctors, different hospitals - whatever we need to do, I'm willing to help to see, um, my son recover."

He finally took a breath to see what this understanding woman was thinking.

"First of all you can call us Katy and Les. We're family, even though we're just meeting." Katy smiled and reached out and touched Rafe's hand.

"We do have insurance, but we do appreciate any additional help," She continued once she saw that he understood what she was saying. "Realistically, we have asked the doctors what can be done. They have investigated the possibilities and right now Cyrus is strong. He's merely caught in this 'other world' and needs to find his way home. Could I ask for something instead? Would you pray with me, Rafe?"

She gave him a playful wink and squeezed his hand.

"Yes, prayer I can do, Mrs. Fre... Katy. That I can do."

He held her hand and they all bowed their heads.

***

As I looked at the man I had come to know so well over my journey, I was struck with an awareness that the royal figure before me had always carried himself with this persona. Even during the brutal fight sequence, as I thought back, Elijah had looked upon me with love and compassion.

Now as he sat between the other kings and queens, an unexpected clap of thunder and lightning lit up the grand hall. The light seemed to make his crown and skin glisten like they were accented with gold. That was when I realized that my friend was looking straight at me. Despite the familiarity, his gaze caused me to immediately bow lower and look away.

"Master Cyrus, please come forward."

Elijah spoke in this realm with a power that reverberated through the room, bordering on a roar, and caused me to shake with a fear I had never felt at any other point of my time with him. I looked around to see if the king was speaking to me and then I carefully raised my eyes to look at the thrones.

"Yes, you Cyrus Rover. Step forward." The intimacy and commanding tone lifted me to my feet.

"Yes...um...sir?"

I walked up to the top step of the staging area. Then I did the only thing that came naturally to me at that moment, I knelt down in reverence.

"Yes, sir," I repeated.

"Master Cyrus, your presence has been made known to us," said a different voice. "You have ridden on the honorable steed, Fireinder, and she has shared your story with us. Yet, we long to hear how you came to be in Asaph."

As the person spoke, I looked to see who was talking to him. One of the queens was asking me to share my story. Despite having a distinctly English accent, her tone and inflection sounded like Mika. This helped to calm my thoughts and to be drawn by her query.

"Yes, um... your highness? Sorry, I'm not familiar with your name. Are you asking me to share my story with the court?"

"My apologies, Master Cyrus," she smiled. "I am sister to the king, Queen Fanon and yes, the court would be entertained and interested in your tales of adventure. They sound familiar to my siblings and I, and familiar to our past. Also, they may help us to know how we can help you to get home. Can you share with us your journey?"

She motioned towards the center of the stage.

"Ah, yes, but Queen Fanon, this will all seem quite odd to everyone here," I admitted. "Still, I'm willing to share, especially if it means finding a means of finding the key for my father and getting home. Do you want me to share it with everyone here?"

I pointed to the spot she had motioned to and walked toward her. Her smile was even reminiscent of Mika's cheeky grin.

"Oh, what fun," she said, clapping her hands and motioning to the crowd. "Please take a seat everyone. Servants, please serve the guests drinks and sustenance. Master Cyrus, do you need a chair or would you prefer to stand?"

I wasn't ready for a full-blown presentation of this life but, as a storyteller of sorts, I would do my best. Admittedly, this had to be the most bizarre audience I had ever faced in my life. Animals, mythical creatures and royalty. Needless to say, I felt the pressure, especially as the kings and queens moved to chairs in front of the crowd. Then something odd occurred that changed my whole demeanor.

"Master Cyrus, just tell your story," Elijah said as I walked past him. "You will bless all, and it will open the door to the possibilities of you returning home. Remember the words - the door, the key and the doorkeeper are the same."

As I looked at my friend, the king, I saw a key around his neck. That is when he reached out and touched my shoulder. His touch gave me a short burst of energy that electrified my body and mind. Suddenly, I had the confidence, courage, and stamina to share my story. The king took his place in the audience, and I began my tale of adventure. What could have been one of the scariest experiences in my life turned out to be one of the most invigorating.

"Yes, Queen Fanon and guests, I would be honored to share my journey to this fair land. It is best told in the standing position. Prepare to be amazed, terrified, and dazzled, because even I cannot explain how this all came to be."

I winked at the crowd and started with my last thoughts before hitting the side of the delivery van. I only had a little over a day left before the time was up for this journey. Why not share the story?

***

I guess I didn't disappoint. The audience was entranced throughout the whole presentation. The squirrels had to be quieted occasionally as they asked for clarification of characters – "Who is Mika? Why did they throw stones? What is a bicycle?"

After the encouragement from the king, I was animated and engaging from chapter to chapter. The servants would bring me drinks and food periodically, but no one seemed too weary of my anecdotes. As I came to the end, the crowd was genuinely disappointed.

"As I looked back," I finished, "I was jettisoned into your world and found myself face to face with the noble, yet terrifying war horse, Ardan. Now I find myself before one of the most captivating and royal audiences as I look ahead to the next chapter of this adventure."

As I said these words, I finally sat on the chair the servants had brought on the stage. There was a pause, and the silence was deafening. Then the room erupted. The kings and queens stood, and the crowd cheered.

"Cyrus! Cyrus!"

There was a dull roar about the space that mystified and pleased him. That was when King Elijah ascended the stairs to the stage and stood next to me. I stood and tried to look respectful. I must have seemed to be pondering whether to bow when the king spoke.

"Master Cyrus, you have been on quite a quest. It seems The Maker wants you to learn something about yourself and your world."

He paused, and there was a soft, reverent tone in his voice as he said The Maker's name.

"Master Cyrus," the king said, looking me in the eyes, "you have told the story well. Also, this will be your final chapter, but it will not be without difficulty and may be the end for you, too."

I went from elation to fear in seconds. The end?

"Yes, my son, your final chapter of this adventure must end with a battle. It is the one you have been preparing for throughout this quest. Tomorrow at dawn, you must battle the Black Knight. Your time is coming to a close on this adventure of discovery. The outcome of this fight will determine your fate. He is a fierce competitor, and it will not be easy, but I feel you are ready for this duel."

King Elijah then turned to the crowd.

"Now, as witnesses, kings, queens, people, and noble creatures of Asaph, you will meet at the great battleground at dawn to see how our Master Cyrus will fare against the worthy challenger, the Black Knight," he announced. "This is what you have been working towards throughout this quest, Cyrus. Until then, eat, drink, and rest. For tomorrow will be the great battle of Cyrus Rover."

When he finished, the crowd cheered and slowly dispersed from the Grand Hall.

I just sat there until the room was empty. The only one who remained was Elijah. He looked around, took off his crown and then did something very unroyal. He hugged me.

"My friend, The Maker has been sifting you and preparing you for this day," he said, holding me at arm's length. "You need to fight. The result will be the reward of either returning home or to Your Maker. Either one has its benefits. Also, this battle will make evident how you can set your father free. Tonight, study the map you have been given and rest. Eat well in the morning, and I will see you at the battleground outside the castle."

As he finished, a young elf approached and motioned for me to follow him.

"Elijah... I mean, Your Majesty, could I die tomorrow?"

I stood there dumbfounded and exhausted.

"Master Cyrus," the king said, "read the map, get some rest, and all will be made clear in the morning."

He looked at the elf.

"Nathaniel please see our guest to his room."

Then he winked at me.

"Cy, all will be made clear in the morning."

I walked away in a trance until the elf spoke.

"Master Cyrus, you are a wonderful storyteller. Trust King Elijah. Trust The Maker. Let's get you to your room. It's a big day tomorrow. You must get your rest."

21

To The Death?

Sleep eluded me. I was given a room with all the luxuries you'd expect in a magical land like Asaph. Food, drink, a luxurious bed, and access to servants who would bring the guest anything he needed. Before leaving him in his room, Nathaniel had shown me everything he could get to help me relax.

"The royals want to ensure you have anything you desire," the elf said. "If you can think of something, merely pull that rope. Someone will be here instantly. Can I do anything for you, Master Cyrus?"

"Honestly, do you want to be my second in the battle tomorrow and fight this Black Knight?" I answered, settling back into a huge velvet-lined chair. "But seriously, can you tell me anything about this man?"

Nathaniel took a few grapes and came across the room.

"Ha! I can't fight this battle for you, this is your fight. Still, all I can tell you about your foe is that he is legendary. The Black Knight can mirror his opponent and is nearly impossible to defeat."

"Yeah, thanks. Not sure that's what I need to hear right now, Nate."

I seemed to get sucked into the chair as I considered the battle. Without warning, the elf stood before me.

"Okay, Cyrus, snap out of it," he ordered. "King Elijah has given you your instructions. He does not treat these things lightly and would not put you in the battle ring if there wasn't an assurance that you could win. So, stop feeling sorry for yourself and do as the king told you to do. Pray to The Maker and get some sleep. Do you understand me, young Master?"

His look was unnerving and reassuring at the same time. This caused me to sit up and look around the room for my things. That was when I noticed that they were all neatly put on a table across from my bed.

"Okay, Nate. I guess that is what I do have working for me. Anything else?"

"Nate? I kind of like that. You can call me Nate," the elf said. "No, King Elijah's words are always enough," he assured me. "Follow his instructions and trust that The Maker will guide you. That is all. Now, I will leave you to it. Go well."

The elf bowed to honor me, then snapped his fingers, turned, and bounded gracefully out of the room.

These marching orders caused me to become very aware of the reality of the situation and that there was no going back. My father and his life depended on my response to this challenge. The first thing I needed to do was to inventory all I had in my bag to determine what I had for the battle. The map was back to looking like it did when it was handed to me at the beginning of the journey. Sigil was now a beautiful, hand-crafted sword. It had the head of a lion etched into the blade and the number 617 under the animal's image. My jacket was folded on the table as a coat of silver chainmail. I had worn something like it in a play in high school. It was light but felt strong enough. The belt was still around my waist. It had a place to hold my sword and had an ornate design cut into the leather. The reliable hat was now a helmet of unrecognizable metal. The armor had the same lion inscription etched into the back with the number 617 inscribed on its forehead. I hoped the shoes would help me to keep my balance during this battle. Finally, as I took the last item out of the bag, the backpack transformed into a shield. It was magnificent and beautifully designed. As I lifted it off the table, I was amazed at how light it was. It was interesting that I felt a certain amount of comfort in my armor, but I still had no way of knowing how to go about fighting someone who was a legendary warrior.

"Well, map," I said. "You're all I've got. What do you have to tell me?"

I set my gear to the side, grabbed the map and rolled it onto the table. I could see that the line that showed my journey had come to the map's edge. On the page were two swords. Under the swords was something I hadn't seen before. A small flap was cut into the page like those in children's books that showed something under the flap. I lifted the flap and underneath, there were these words written in ancient script:

Man may not live on bread alone. Yet, today every word you need from The Maker will come through the bread. Find the cross, you will find the answers you seek.

"Find the cross – what does that mean? The bread?"

My curiosity was piqued, but I wasn't sure what this cryptic expression meant. Cross? Bread? I kept it running through my mind. Then I looked across the table and saw the food left behind by the castle staff. That was when I saw them, buns with crosses cut into the top. There were about a half dozen spread throughout the bread options. I sat up and reached the basket and pulled it to me.

"What the hell, what do I have to lose?"

Without much thought, I grabbed the first bun and took a bite. There wasn't too much to the act except that they were delicious. As I chewed, my hand seemed to have a mind of its own and it reached out to Sigil. The sword came to life, and I started to swipe the air with a proficiency that only magic could explain. This motivated me to eat all of the buns, and with each bite, I found I acquired skills I didn't have before. My feet, hands, and body worked in ways that surprised and excited me simultaneously. Before I knew it, the night was fading behind me. Rest was the next thing on the agenda. I went back to the map and saw another flap. Under this one there was another inscription:

The Maker makes everything, his safety and rest come through the wine. Lie down and sleep in safety.

Granted, I was exhausted after going through a Matrix-like experience of gaining training on sword play. It was late and I needed some sleep. Yet, before I poured a glass of wine, I noticed one more flap on the map. It was marked with the word, final instruction. I went around the table, poured myself a glass of wine, and then returned to the map before taking a drink. Under the small piece of paper, these words were written:

Listen to The Maker and present your bodies as a living sacrifice. This is how you will show honor and enter into His presence. The key to life is to lose it.

"What?"

I was exasperated and tired. I pondered these final words and, without thinking, quenched my thirst. The next thing I remember was hearing the voice of Nathaniel. The elf was trying to wake me.

"Master Cyrus! It's Nate. Wake up, the time has come for the battle."

***

Rafe had gone to get some coffee for Katy and Les. As he entered the room, Katy was holding Cyrus' hand. Les was napping in the corner chair.

"I think I felt him squeeze my hand, Rafe," Katy said, whispering so she wouldn't wake her husband. "Come see if you can feel it."

She motioned with her head towards Cy's other hand. The father sat beside his son, and set the coffee on the small table beside the bed. He reached out for his son's hand. Despite being in a cast, Rafe thought he felt a slight squeeze at that moment. His eyes widened.

"I think I felt something," he whispered back. "Should we call the doctor?"

"I already pressed the call button," Katy replied. "I'm sorry, but there is no way I'm letting go of my grandson's hand now, Rafe. I'm praying. The medical team will have to work around me."

She smiled and then bowed her head and prayed. All Rafe could do was pray too, even as Radke and the team came in to see what was wrong. Katy told them what had happened, then she went back to praying. The medical team chose not to force the grandmother to move. Radke looked to Rafe.

"Mr Rover, we need one arm. Can I ask you..."

"Sure, sure," he said, getting up.

He grabbed his coffee and stepped to the back of the room. The team worked around Cyrus, but did all they could to respect Katy as she prayed. When they finished, Rafke came over to Rafe.

"Mr Rover, your son is fine, but his heart rate has increased. There is no way to know why, but we will monitor him for now. Signal us if there are any changes. I'll be back to check on him in an hour or so. Keep praying. Let's see what happens.'

The nurse reached out and squeezed the man's hand.

"I will, I will. And thank you."

Rafe sat on the other side of the bed and started praying. As things settled in the room, Les remained sleeping in the corner.

***

As we walked up to the field that Nathaniel led me to, I could see a massive crowd surrounding the grounds. All kinds of creatures were in attendance. Bears, beavers, the Minotaur, elves and huge men who looked like giants. Despite the reception and cheers from some who saw the young man arriving, the audience members I could not miss were the royal family and King Elijah. They were sitting in a grandstand that was covered with a beautiful tent-like structure. Flags flew over the top and once they saw me, trumpets sounded from somewhere in the area of the tent. That was when the crowd roared with excitement and, as I entered the battleground, I saw him.

The Black Knight stood in the middle of the ground. He wore a helmet and armor that shone despite barely any sunlight. On his back was a shield, but the sword he held in front of him was impressive. Like his armor, the blade looked like a black metal that seemed to throb with the rising sun's light. He was terrifying and captivating at the same time. Yet, he stood without moving, making the cheers go quiet as everyone saw the warrior and things turned into a hushed awe.

All I could do was stare at my potential adversary as I walked onto the battlefield. Since I wasn't paying attention to my surroundings, I ran into Nathaniel who had stopped to bow to the royal box. I almost fell over the elf.

"Ugh. oh, so sorry, Nate. Sorry," the words came out as I collided with the young elf.

My armor clanged together as I tried to collect myself and do an honorable bow. All I could do was perform an exaggerated kneeling action and say, "Your Highnesses."

Queen Fanon giggled, but no one else seemed impressed. At that moment, King Elijah came to the front of the stage.

"Good citizens of Asaph, you are here to witness the final battle of Cyrus, master storyteller and warrior."

The crowd cheered, but just as quickly went silent as the King continued.

"Today, at dawn, Master Cyrus must discover the purpose of this journey. Hear me now. Unless a grain of wheat falls into the earth and dies, it remains alone; but if it dies, it bears much fruit. The only way for Cyrus to be released and to find the key is to fight to the death."

King Elijah looked to the knight on the field.

"Today's battle is with the Black Knight. Please present yourself, good sir."

The man moved towards the royal box. He walked with a confidence and swagger that captured every eye in the crowd. As he arrived at the stage, he knelt and bowed before the royal entourage. Then he stood, tipped his head to Cyrus, and removed his helmet.

Suddenly, I was looking at an identical image of myself – no variation except his ominously opulent armor. It was me; I was going to be fighting myself. What was happening? Could I be any more confused?

Discover the Third Space Discussion Guide that complements this chapter and join Cyrus Rover on his journey. You'll find the QR code to access them at the beginning of the book with the "Free Gift".

22

— · —

IS THIS THE END?

As they prayed, Rafe and Katy felt Cyrus squeeze their hands simultaneously. Each looked over at the other. Instead of calling for the hospital staff this time, they smiled and prayed.

***

"Hello Cyrus Rover."

The Black Knight stood and kept looking at me. Confidently, he tucked his helmet under his arm.

"Are you ready for the fight of your life?"

"Who are you?" I asked as I looked at my twin.

I struggled to get my bearings but did my best to stand eye-to-eye with the black-clad warrior.

"Haven't you figured it out yet? I'm you. We represent different sides of the same person. I know what you have been through to get here, but this is the harsh reality of this stage. For you to return to your life in your world, one of us must die. Both of us represent you, but only one of us can survive. This isn't a dream," the Black Knight assured me. "You have entered the battlefield for your future. Yet, the trick is figuring out which of us must die. There's no way for both of us to exist, but which of us must die for the other to live? This is your final test."

With that, he put his helmet back on and walked to the middle of the battlefield. The Black Knight stood there glistening in the morning sun as he pulled out his beautiful sword and lifted his shield off of his back. He was ready for battle.

"Come, Cyrus Rover. Come."

What is going on? I wondered. My thoughts were running wild, 'One of us must die?' What was going on? Come on, wake up, Cyrus. I kept saying this to myself. Wake Up!

But all I could do was stand there in disbelief. I looked at the Black Knight; then I looked back at the royals. The crowd had started a chant for the battle to begin. That was when I caught the eye of Elijah. The King held up his hand and the crowd stopped.

"Master Cyrus, you must fight the good fight," he called. "You've been trained. The rounds will go on for five minutes and not end until one of you has given his life. The victor will receive the freedom and the burden of the other person."

"You will both have your support team in your corners," the King spoke, "but the final words I can offer you is to know that those who save their lives will lose it, but whoever loses his life for The Maker and his message will save it. Now, the battle must begin."

Upon that command, I heard a clatter of metal behind me, and I was barely able to duck under the blade of The Black Knight as it swept over my head. The battle had begun.

***

A shudder ran through Cyrus' body, making him move for the first time with any sort of significance since arriving at the hospital. That was enough for Rafe to push the button for the staff to come, but all Katy did was double down on her prayers.

"Oh Lord, save our Cyrus. Save him.'"

***

As I stumbled away from my pursuing foe, I got my helmet on and my sword out. I was terrified, but something within my soul caused me to step back into the fray instead of running. All I had learned through the night gave me fresh confidence and awareness of my skills. I could feel the power of The Spirit running through my veins.

***

Cyrus' arms went rigid. He squeezed both of his family members' hands hard.

"Ouch," Rafe said, almost pulling his hand away. "What just happened?"

"Keep praying, Rafe," Grandma Katy said. "Don't stop, don't let go."

Rafe nodded his head, but still reached out and pushed the button again to signal the staff with his other hand. Then he bowed and prayed.

***

It was like nature understood the significance of this battle. Lightning struck and cracked open the sky. I stepped back into the fray with the knight. That was when the crowd erupted, and the fight was on.

Since we were equally matched, the battle was intense. It was bizarre to watch. We seemed to energize one another. As our swords hit, the crowd would cheer. When fists hit their target, the audience jumped to their feet. Then the horns blew and the first round was over. The rounds went on throughout the morning and as they came to the end of the fifth, we both went to their corners again.

As I returned, Nathaniel brought over a drink. I was surprisingly supercharged, but I showed concern in my eyes.

"Wow, Nathaniel, this is exciting," I said, turning to the elf. "I never knew I could do any of this for so long and still feel like I could go all day. But..."

"But?" Nathaniel said, listening.

"Um, we're perfectly matched. How do I win?" I asked. "Also, I don't want to kill anyone, especially someone who, well, is me. What do I do?"

I drank the drink and looked at the young elf. He looked back at me.

"Master Cyrus, you could go all day. The crowd would love it, but one thing I do know, you should listen to King Elijah's words. Did you hear? Those who save their lives will lose them, but whoever loses his life for The Maker will save it? It doesn't make sense, but you've been on this journey. What do these words say about this battle?"

***

As the staff checked Cyrus, he seemed to relax. Everyone in the room acknowledged that he seemed to have a contemplative look on his face. Then it suddenly changed and there was a tear going down his cheek. Grandma Katy bowed her head and the tears started flowing down her face, too.

***

At that moment, I knew what to do as the lightning cracked and the horn blew. As I stood, I paused and bowed my head. Then I did something that didn't make sense. I removed my helmet and armor. The shield suddenly turned back into a bag. I took my sword off my belt, and Sigli reappeared, and I put it in my bag, then I placed my bag in the corner. This left me entirely exposed.

A palpable hush fell over the crowd. The tone was completely different than the first round as the land's latest champion walked into the ring. The Black Knight stood stoically and grandly. His sword in front of him, his shield on his back and the midday light made him look majestic. I approached my adversary.

"Let's finish this for both of us," I said. "This has been one of my greatest experiences in life, but I have to step out and have faith that this is the right choice. You have been an overwhelming foe, but this is where it must end. This is something Pastor Hudson used to say to me. I've got to surrender my life to God. You'd call him The Maker. So, here it goes."

The Black Knight looked confused, but I didn't care about what he thought.

"Today I commit my life to The Maker and trust him with all of my life," I continued. "I can no longer fight; my life is now in His hands. I surrender myself and sacrifice my own life. In the name of The Maker, take it."

The knight didn't hesitate. He didn't say a word. He lifted his sword and buried it in my body. As he pulled it out, no sound was heard around the field. I stood for a moment, peace coming over my face, followed by a small smile, and then I fell to my knees. I remained on my knees and bowed my head. Everything went black.

The battle was over.

***

Just as things were starting to happen in the hospital room, Cyrus' vitals crashed within a moment and the monitors showed that his heart had stopped. Every member of the crash team came in and attempted to do everything they could to revive him.

Rafe went to the corner where Katy had been moved. They hugged one another and tried not to watch everything going on in the room that was happening to their boy. That is when the pair noticed Mika in the doorway. Even though Rafe didn't know Cyrus' friend, he signaled for her to approach them. Katy explained what was happening as they huddled in the corner of the room to stay out of the way of the medical team. Les grabbed Katie's hand. This is when they started to pray again.

***

The Black Knight walked away, tipping his helmet to his fallen foe. Cyrus remained kneeling in the field as the lightning shattered the sky. Then the sun broke through the clouds and a beam of light shone down on his humble body.

At that moment, a shadow crept across the field. King Elijah walked across the field. As he came upon the young man, the king stopped in front of Cyrus' body.

"Master Cyrus," he said, speaking as though the young man could hear. "Few people who travel on your journey fully understand what you grasped so quickly. Your maturity was a joy to watch grow. The Maker has done a work in you. You discovered the truth that living your life meant dieing to yourself. Master Cyrus, you have been set free, and now, as a new creature. Your choice, your sacrifice, has given you the key to your father's freedom. This sacrifice was for your soul, but it also rippled through time and breaks the past bonds that have kept you from your father. One action leading to the freedom of two men. I challenge you to see this gift as a new beginning for the rest of your life."

As Elijah finished speaking, the king put his hand on the young warrior's shoulder. At that moment, there was a groundswell of cheers from the crowd as Cyrus' body disappeared into the midday beam of light from the sun. It was like the sun poured out a wave that swept across the land with a great force that swept Cyrus' body away like leaves on an autumn day.

The sun sent its light across the land and it burst through the door into the adventurer's cave. Each door on the wall burst open with light that seemed to be accompanied by triumphant music of celebration that was reminiscent of Tchaikovsky's 1812 Overture. As the light traveled out into the cavern and across the bridge, this once dingy and terrifying underground world turned into a vestibule of sight and sound. The music reverberated off the walls and the bridge reflected the beauty of the light with a magnificent radiance. Then the sunrays burst into the gloomy and somber room that housed the imprisoned vision of Cyrus' father. Suddenly the force and chains that were holding the man in the chair disintegrated and the man's body was swept away into the rays of the sun. Yet, this rush of light continued forward through each door that Cyrus had entered. The orchestral presence jettisoned through the worlds of the academy of mutants, through the Spunk Café, down the stairs of the Irish pub, passed by the wing-backed chairs and finally came into the private schoolroom where Elijah was sitting at the desk.

***

I suddenly found myself sitting at a desk in front of my friend, my teacher and my mentor. I patted myself where the Black Knight had plunged his sword into my body. All I felt was the uniform of the school and no wound.

"Wait, wait. I'm alive? What happened?"

I was elated, but so confused.

Elijah smiled.

"You found the key, Cyrus. First it was trusting The Maker, then finally realizing this journey was one of sacrifice and discovery. The key was with me and The Maker. Now you and your father are free."

He put my bag on my desk.

"This is the way you will remember your experiences here. Now, go live your life for The Maker, Cyrus Rover."

I stood up and hugged the man who had been my guide through this journey. His embrace was encouraging and comforting. After I let go of Elijah, I grabbed the bag and put it on my back.

"Thank you, King Elijah. You've given me a new life. I hope I can make the most of this gift. Thank you, my friend."

As I finished, I thought I saw a tear in Elijah's eye.

In that instant, the light swept through the room like an unavoidable wave of the ocean.

***

I abruptly awoke in the hospital room. The medical team stopped working and all looked at one another with astonishment.

"Did you do something different?" Radka asked. "What happened?"

Everyone went quiet. Sylvia looked at the nurse and could only shrug her shoulders.

I had tubes all over me, but I could see Grandma Katy, Grandpa Les, Mika, and a man standing in the corner praying. There was a beam of sunlight shining through the window onto the stranger.

All I could think was, who's that guy? Then I took a moment to reach down to where the sword had gone through my chest. There was no wound or injury and all I could do was give a long sigh of relief.

Before I laid my head back down, I noticed a chair next to the four people praying. In it was my bag from the journey. It was a bit worn and muddied, but the mere sight of it brought me comfort. All I could do was smile and lay back in the bed.

Thank The Maker, I'm home, I thought. What a story I have to tell.

23

THE NEXT QUEST BEGINS

'The unfolding of your words gives light; it imparts understanding to the simple.'

Everything seemed different from that moment on in my life. It took me a few days to finally leave the hospital, but this gave me time to come to terms with all that happened while I was in a coma. Life was different for me. Nothing looked the same since I died and came back to life. Some people would never believe my story, my quest, and I can understand it is hard to comprehend. Interestingly, six people believed me, because they had been through it with me. Doctor Bloodworth, Nurse Radka, Grandma Katy, Grandpa Les, Mika, and Rafe Rover, the renowned and celebrated cinematographer – and my father.

When I finally did leave the hospital, Nurse Radka and the staff threw a celebration. They gave me balloons, cake, and a pendant that could hang on my bag.

The seasoned nurse gently hugged me.

"We'll never forget you, Cyrus," she said. "You may have been a quiet patient, but you caused more turmoil than you were worth. Yet, I think your family and friends have blessed us all. Also, we all hope that we might be in one of your movies in the future."

She winked, and the team laughed.

"Thanks, Radka, and to you all.," I said. "I'm thankful to be here and hope this experience won't be for nothing. You helped me to become a new man, and I promise to live this life to the fullest. I'm grateful to you all and to The Maker – or for a better understanding, Jesus, for this time."

I lifted my juice cup as a means of honoring the team.

The celebration broke up soon after the speeches as the department had to respond to admitting new patients. Nurse Radka and some of the doctors shook my hand, and then one of the hospital volunteers offered to take me to the front door. The wheelchair wasn't really necessary, but it was hospital policy.

"Hey, Cy, stay clear of delivery vans in that chair!" one of the nurses said.

There were a few laughs as I headed towards the elevator with my grandparents. My father had gone down to bring his car around. As we got to the front door, I was surprised to have the volunteer pushing his chair touch me on the shoulder and whisper in my ear.

"Master Cyrus, this is when the journey begins, don't forget what you've been given," said a familiar voice. "Go well, my friend."

I jumped up and spun around. There was a man there I didn't recognise. I looked into his eyes. I grabbed my backpack.

"Excuse me, what did you say?"

His voice sounded familiar and as my eyes adjusted, I thought the man looked familiar. "Oh, nothing sir, but I wish you well, Master Cyrus. Take care and live well."

He winked, turned, and pushed the wheelchair away, whistling Tchaikovsky's 1812 Overture.

24

····•····

EPILOGUE

Rafe Rover

My dad seemed to want to make up for lost time. After my recovery, he took me to Australia to be with him as he finished his latest production. It was like a dream come true to be with this man. Every free moment we had was spent getting to know one another. He listened to me and quietly shared his thoughts. The most significant moment during our trip down under was when he asked for forgiveness for not being there for my mother and me. Honestly, I held no animosity towards the man. I was so thrilled to have him in my life, there was nothing I could think to hold against him. My life had been good up to this point; this only made it better.

Dad returned with me to the film school to give a few talks. Then he left me there to finish my degree. He wanted me to earn my way independently, and I respected that. But that wasn't his exit. Not in the least bit. We had found one another, and both of us would work to become a family.

Tyler Smith

You may not remember the story from Pastor Hudson, but I did reach out to Tyler after my recovery. We caught up whenever I came home. I shared some of my projects with him and we went to see a few movies together. Yet, the most significant thing was that he started going back to the youth group. It took time and he still went through some tough times at home, but eventually he decided to become a Christian. It changed his life and that of his family. Guess what? Tyler is currently serving as the youth pastor and still loves all things Star Wars.

Grandma and Grandpa Fremont

My grandparents went back to life. They enjoyed the simplicity of their lives but admitted that the highlights came when I was on break and chose to go home. Rafe did fly them out to California regularly to join me on some West Coast trips. It was special, but they never really felt comfortable in that world. Yet, they loved seeing me soaking it all in out there.

One thing they did every night was pray for my dad and me. Their family had grown, and they needed to commit their 'boys' to the Lord. They knew their worlds would never be the same, but they learned who to trust with this unknown future. Their Lord would watch over this new season we were all traveling through.

Mika

Upon waking up from my quest, one of the first things I did was kiss this beautiful woman and invest in our relationship. We became more than friends. What always made me stop and remember my alternate world was how being around her electrified my life. We talked for days about my story and how this would make a fantastic screenplay. Even though the realities of this coming together were impossible since many of the actors were not even alive anymore. It became a passion for both of us, leading to unique artistic collaborations as the years unfolded.

And this emotional and spiritual aspect of our world spilled over into our relationship. After graduating from film school, we married. Some thought we were too young, but we never doubted our choice. Especially after hearing Rafe's story, we wanted to ensure that history would be different for us.

The Quest

Well, I was driven by the gift from my quest. I never let it go, even when things were at their worst in my life and career. As I studied the journey in detail, I could see what The Maker had been teaching me. Wisdom, justice, the fight, decision-making, sacrifice, forgiveness, family, and mentors were all subjects that were put through biblical scrutiny. I saw how these studies catalysed future projects and personal studies, and strengthened my faith.

Some may wonder if Mika and I made a film about the quest? We're still working on that screenplay and already have a producer who has a keen eye for cinematography. See if it ever makes it to a theater near you.

Until then, what is your quest?

Listen to someone who had to learn the hard way. Don't wait for a delivery truck for The Maker to get a hold of your life. I challenge you to see this gift given to me as a new beginning that could impact the rest of your life.

THE LOST CHAPTER

In this 'lost chapter' discover the beginnings of a new story...

Unlock instant access to The Lost Chapter, where another story is about to begin by visiting https://thirdspace.org.au/lostchapteror scanning the QR code below.

ACKNOWLEDGEMENTS

Movies can speak to so many areas of our lives. Different genres, characters, and eras provide a fascinating collection of cultural engagement. *The Maker's Quest* taps into the value of great mentors represented on screen. This adventure shows how they helped Cyrus Rover on his spiritual journey.

This book is meant to complement the work of City Bible Forum / Third Space's work that inspired and motivated these works.

To honor those who have mentored me over the years, I want to thank all who have come alongside me and supported my development in ministry, work, and life.

Ministry mentors: Craig Josling, Peter Kaldor, Steve Mayo, Pat Nemmers, and Ben Kwok

Media mentors: Adrian Drayton, Mark Hadley, Ben McEchean & Laura Bennett

Family: Ron & Delores Matthews, Mitch Matthews & Clayton Fisher

The spark in my life: Cathy, whenever you hold my hand, sit with me over dinner, or merely walk into the room, you electrify my life. Your love, support, care, patience, encouragement, and faith are an example for all who know you, but I relish that you are my wife, friend, and lover. Remember that I love you, Cath.

Ultimate mentor: Jesus is the inspiration for the ministry of *Reel Dialogue* and the books that continue to come from this discussion of film and faith. My hope is that this book and ministry glorify my Savior. As my primary mentor and inspiration, thank you for the motivation and direction, especially for my salvation.

ABOUT THE AUTHOR

Russ Matthews works as a team member of City Bible Forum, Third Space, and ABWE ministries in Sydney, Australia.

One of his key roles is managing the ministry of Reel Dialogue. He writes film reviews and articles for Reel Dialogue which are published in various publications.

Russ has a passion for film and getting conversations started on themes from these visual creations. The discussions can include topics of life's bigger questions that can include God, the Bible, and Jesus.

Russ is married to Cathy, and they enjoy spending as much time with their children, grandchildren, and family as possible.